TO WIN A FROZEN HEART

CLARA WINFIELD

First published 2018 by Heartiman

First published in paperback 2018 by Heartiman

Copyright © Clara Winfield 2018

and without a similar condition including this condition
being imposed on the subsequent purchaser.

Dedicated to A Lady, with love and gratitude

AUTHOR'S NOTE

To Win a Frozen Heart is set in the world of Jane Austen's *Pride and Prejudice*, using Miss Austen's own characters.

A handful of side characters have been devised especially for this story and do not appear in Miss Austen's original text.

This book is written in British English, using British English spellings and grammar.

CHAPTER 1

"Do stop fussing, Lizzy. I am not in need of a nurse just yet."

Elizabeth adjusted Mr. Bennet's pillows anyway. She stood back then and surveyed the frail old man before her.

"Very well, Father. I shall leave you to read in peace. But be sure to ring the bell if you need anything. I have instructed the servants to fetch me at once, if you should feel—" She hesitated. "If your health worsens."

"Fiddlesticks. I shall be up and about in no time, Lizzy. Mark my words. You know, I've never had a day's illness in my life. This chill will pass quickly."

Mr. Bennet opened his leather-bound book and turned his attention away from his daughter.

He had always prided himself on having a strong constitution, capable of repelling any malady. Indeed, he frequently insisted to his family that he had never succumbed to a single cough or cold since the day he was born.

Elizabeth doubted the truth of this, and rather suspected his memory had grown hazy over the years. Yet it was certainly true that her father had never been restricted to his bed by the doctor before. Neither had Mr. Bennet ever found the simple tasks of daily life difficult, until that morning three weeks ago, when Kitty had found him lying on his side on the sitting-room rug. He had explained that he had been on his way to sit by the fire, and had tripped over something. Yet Elizabeth had checked the room afterwards, and had found no hazard that could have tripped him.

As she reached the doorway, her father called after her.

"Whatever you do, don't let Mary come upstairs and sing to me again. If anything is likely to finish me off, it will be one of Mary's tuneless arias."

"I shall do my best to dissuade her," Elizabeth said, closing the door behind her with a smile.

Downstairs, a welcome surprise awaited her in the drawing room.

"Jane! How wonderful to see you again so soon!"

The sisters embraced. Elizabeth immediately felt the cares of the day lifting off her. It was always pleasing to see her beloved Jane. The Bennets and the Bingleys had celebrated the New Year together just two days ago, but Jane and Elizabeth still had plenty to talk about. They always did.

"Mr. Bingley is attending to some business on the estate, so I took the chaise on a whim. I had been hoping for an opportunity to see you once again, my dear Lizzy. I had hoped we might find a quiet spot for a conversation."

"And I am very glad you came. Shall we take a stroll around the gardens?"

Jane laughed. "Heavens, no! The north wind is bitingly cold today. Much too cold for a walk."

"Is it?" Elizabeth glanced out of the window. She hadn't noticed the iron-grey sky and the bending of the young tree saplings. Now she saw what her sister meant. As she turned back from the window, she caught Jane frowning.

"If another of us should fall ill this week, it would be a disaster."

Elizabeth turned this statement over in her mind. "It would be unfortunate during any week, surely?"

"Oh, Lizzy." Jane took her sister's hand. "Have you forgotten so soon? The Twelfth Night ball is in three days' time. It will be my first ball as the lady of the house. And it is to be our last social event at Netherfield before we return to London for the remainder of the winter. I really must be in full health to undertake my duties as hostess." Jane looked at her lap, her face troubled. "In truth, I am somewhat nervous about the responsibility. There is much to oversee."

Elizabeth squeezed Jane's hand and shot her an apologetic look. "Forgive me, Jane. I do not know how I could have forgotten. Please do not worry, though. The ball will run like clockwork. I'm sure of it."

"You are distracted with domestic matters, are you not?" Jane smoothed one of Elizabeth's more unruly curls off her face. "It must be very different at Longbourn with just three sisters remaining. I expect Mary and Kitty look to you for all sorts of help and advice."

Elizabeth sighed. "Hardly. Mary and Kitty think I am a boring old maid with no sense of humour. They choose not to spend much time in my company these days. Plenty of giggling girls their own age in Meryton to talk to, you see."

"They must miss Lydia."

"They do. We all do." Elizabeth's nagging sense of worry about Lydia grew stronger each hour that they did not hear from her. "She is a silly girl at times, but she has never failed to return on time from a friend's house before. We are told she is travelling in their company and just omitted to ask Father's proper permission, but it is unsettling. At some point, we may need to send someone to find and retrieve her."

"And Father? Is the doctor still concerned about him?"

"Yes. I'm afraid Father is sicker than he admits. And Mamma is still in a foul temper about Lydia. She has not left her bedchamber since we returned from Netherfield on New Year's Day."

"Oh dear. Is Mamma sick, as well as furious?"

Elizabeth gave a wry smile. "No. I think she just wants to demonstrate to the whole village how terribly she takes the news of Lydia's escape."

"Escape! Lizzy, you make it sound as though you are all living in a prison."

Elizabeth pondered this. "Well, I suppose I don't feel entirely at liberty. I cannot avoid thinking about what will happen to the family if Father—" She could not finish.

Jane understood. She took her sister's hand, and gave it a squeeze.

"Try not to think of that, dearest Lizzy. Father is far too stubborn to give in to any disease. I'm sure he will recover swiftly. And Mother will soon come to terms with Lydia's irresponsible behaviour, once she returns, and will resume her normal activities."

"I hope so." Elizabeth settled down by the fireside with Jane. "Now tell me all about married life, Mrs. Bingley. We could not speak privately two days ago. I simply must hear everything."

Jane's cheeks flushed a little. "It is most agree-able, Lizzy."

"And three months on, is Mr. Bingley every-thing you hoped he would be?"

"Everything and more."

Jane's eyes sparkled when she spoke of her new husband. Elizabeth wondered if she would ever meet a gentleman who made her eyes sparkle like that. She could not imagine it.

"Have Mr. Bingley's sisters been at Netherfield this week?"

"No. The Hursts have no plans to come down to the country for Twelfth Night, as far as I know. And Miss Bingley prefers to remain in London whenever possible. I do not know if any of them will attend the Netherfield ball. They have not notified me of their intentions."

The sisters exchanged a look. Mrs. Hurst and Miss Bingley could be difficult, and Elizabeth was glad to hear that Jane would not be required to deal with them too frequently in daily life.

"Well, that is all for the best, I am sure."

"Yes, it probably is. We have plenty to do, and many guests arriving over the next two days. This evening, we have visitors arriving from Derbyshire."

"Indeed? Are they friends of Mr. Bingley?"

"Yes. A gentleman and his sister, named Mr. and Miss Darcy. Mr. Bingley speaks so highly of Mr. Darcy that I am sure he will make excellent company. The Darcys will remain at Netherfield for the ball, and then we shall all travel back to London together. It will be splendid."

"If Mr. Darcy happens to be an unmarried gentleman, you had better keep him away from Mary. She is convinced she is to be the next Bennet sister to be wed. I rather think she has dismissed me as a hopeless case."

They laughed.

"On the contrary, Lizzy. I wondered if perhaps Mr. Darcy might turn out to be a suitable match for *you*."

Elizabeth was astonished, and quite forgot what else she had meant to ask her sister. "Goodness, Jane! I have yet to meet the man. Have *you* even been introduced to the Darcys?"

"Not yet. But if my husband favours Mr. Darcy, I am inclined to think him a very pleasant fellow indeed. And there is the small matter of his fortune." She cleared her throat, as though bashful for a moment. "I know you do not care for talk of money, and ordinarily neither do I. But Mr. Darcy is certainly able to support a wife. That is a consideration worth noting."

Elizabeth looked out of the window again. Light flakes of snow had begun to fall. They did not settle, but melted as they touched the ground. Even without carpeting the lawn, they did bring to Lizzy's attention just how cold it was outside that day.

"I promise I shall be very polite to him when we meet, Jane. And I shall not rule him out completely, if he proves to be an amiable sort. Will that do?"

"Perfect, Lizzy. I could ask for no more." Jane sat forward on the edge of her chair. "I must soon call my maid and return to Netherfield, before this weather gets worse. But there is one other thing I wished to speak to you about, beloved sister."

"What is it?" Elizabeth scanned her sister's face for signs of worry, but there were none. If anything, Jane looked happier than ever.

Jane opened her mouth, then closed it again. She seemed to be having trouble phrasing what she wanted to say. Her hands rested absent-mindedly on her abdomen, as she grappled for words.

Something dawned on Elizabeth. She gasped, and grabbed Jane's hands in her own.

"Jane! You're not... Are you?"

"Possibly," Jane said, unable to hide her smile.

"Are you with child?"

"I believe so," Jane whispered. Tears of joy glinted in the corners of her eyes. "Please do not tell a soul, Lizzy. We cannot make a formal announcement for some time yet."

"Oh, Jane!" Elizabeth leaped from her chair and kissed her sister. She felt tears prickle in her own eyes too.

All Jane had ever wanted was to be a wife and mother, and her dreams were all coming true, one by one. It was such glorious news.

"I am so happy for you," she said, kissing her sister's cheek again. "So very happy. You deserve this joy, Jane. You both do. I promise I will not tell anyone."

"Thank you, dearest Lizzy." Jane looked as though she might burst with happiness. "And I am sure it will not be long before we find you a gentleman of your very own. "

Elizabeth smiled at her sister, but privately she doubted it. She had never received a proposal, and she could not imagine that would change. There were never any suitable single gentlemen around Meryton, or the surrounding areas. Even in London, when visiting her Aunt and Uncle Gardiner, she had very rarely met a man worth talking to for long. If any one of them happened to seem interesting, he soon proved himself to be wholly unsuitable in various other ways. Elizabeth had lost faith in the entire institution of marriage.

For her part, their mother had all but given up hope of Elizabeth marrying. Her younger sisters considered her past her prime. At twenty-one, and with no suitors, they considered that she was already on the shelf. Now it seemed their youngest sister may yet bring shame on the family.

Lydia had disappeared with a female friend, of course, but the whiff of possible scandal lingered over the whole affair. Lydia was not blessed with the most astute common sense. She could easily have been talked into something illicit, and then what? None of the Bennets would put it past her. Thank goodness she did not have a suitor, Elizabeth thought. It would be almost impossible for any of them to seal an engagement while Lydia's whereabouts remained uncertain.

But Elizabeth did not want to spoil Jane's happy mood by disagreeing with her about finding a gentleman of her own.

"Yes, perhaps," she replied at last. "Perhaps I

shall find my own perfect match at Netherfield, Jane. Just as you did."

Jane called her maid up from downstairs and sent her to notify the coachman that they were leaving.

"Oh Lizzy, will you come to Netherfield tomorrow, to help me plan the party games? I shall send a carriage for you at noon, if you agree. It would be most useful to have a second pair of eyes."

"If Father is well enough," Elizabeth said, "and if Mamma can spare me, I should be glad to. But I shall come in our own carriage, for yours may all be needed by your guests."

"As you wish."

The two sisters embraced again.

"Goodbye until tomorrow, Lizzy." Jane's maid slipped her travelling cloak over her shoulders, and she pulled it across herself. "I look forward to spending time with you then." Her eyes shone.

Elizabeth had never seen her sister looking more radiant. She watched from the window as Jane's carriage left the driveway.

The horses' hooves drummed away gradually, as the snow swirled around Longbourn.

CHAPTER 2

The next morning, Mr. Bennet was well enough to leave his bed and read by the fire in the library, with a rug over his lap. At long last, Elizabeth was content to leave the house. She left instructions with the servants to send word to her at Netherfield if she were needed.

Mrs. Bennet remained in her own bedchamber, which adjoined her husband's. Elizabeth wondered how her mother was feeling. It was quite unlike her mother to spend any time at all being quiet and reflective. Perhaps she really was unwell?

After a moment's hesitation, Elizabeth decided to put her head around her mother's door. She would check how Mrs. Bennet was feeling, and gauge whether there was anything to worry about.

Fortunately, she found her mother so talkative and full of righteous indignation at Lydia's behaviour that Elizabeth had no further concerns for her health.

Mary and Kitty agreed they would sit with Mr. Bennet while working on their embroidery, at least until dinner time.

"And Father, you must return to your bed for a rest in the late afternoon. The doctor insisted that you take as much time to recover as you need."

"Very well, dear." Mr. Bennet did not even try to protest. Elizabeth was glad.

"I shall fetch you your choice of book when you awaken," promised Mary.

"That will be lovely," Elizabeth said. "But remember that it is important that we keep Father in a fully relaxed state. For example, you must not excite him with any music." She glanced conspiratorially at her father, whose pale blue eyes twinkled back at her.

Mary nodded solemnly. "Of course. I promise I will follow the doctor's instructions. No music for you, Father, until you are a great deal better. I know you will be sorry for it, but we must make you well again."

Mr. Bennet winked at Elizabeth. "Very well. I shall do my best to bear the disappointment."

As a result of all her preparation, Elizabeth was confident that the household would run smoothly in her absence. The day would pass without a hitch. She was not needed.

When the carriage had been prepared and brought to the front of the house, she felt quite content to climb inside it with her maid. Now she could travel the three miles to Netherfield without worrying about her family.

The weather was still very cold, but the sky was a clear soft blue, and there was no more snow. Crossing the countryside was straightforward, except at one point on a narrow lane when the horses slowed down considerably.

"Is everything all right?" Elizabeth called out to the driver.

"Ice on the road, ma'am. Can't drive the horses too harshly. Won't do no one no good."

"Of course. I quite agree."

Fortunately, the rest of the journey passed without any further hitch. Before long, they were at Netherfield.

Loud chatter rang out from the hallway as Elizabeth and her maid stepped through the heavy oak front door. The house was a whirl of activity. It seemed there were people *everywhere*. Smartly-dressed manservants traipsed up the grand staircase, carrying huge trunks.

Elizabeth passed her cloak to a servant, while her own maid made her way downstairs to the staff quarters.

"Miss Bennet!" called a familiar voice.

It was Miss Bingley, who was back at Netherfield most unexpectedly. Her elder sister Mrs. Hurst was at her side, and so was another young woman Elizabeth did not recognise.

Elizabeth's heart sank. Mr. Bingley's sisters had arrived in time for the ball after all. What a pity.

As always, Miss Bingley and Mrs. Hurst were very smartly dressed, and immaculately groomed. Elizabeth felt they were looking down their noses at her, as they always did. She lifted her chin and gave them the breeziest smile she could manage.

"What a pleasant surprise, Miss Bingley," Elizabeth said. "And Mrs. Hurst too. How lovely to see you both again."

Miss Bingley gave a fleeting, insincere smile. All three women curtseyed, and Miss Bingley pushed forward the unknown young woman.

"Miss Bennet, allow me to present Miss Carrington, of Lincolnshire. Jemima, this is Miss Bennet, Mrs. Bingley's unmarried sister. Now, Miss Bennet lives in a little house three miles hence, all crammed in with her huge family. They manage terribly well, in the circumstances." She gave a tinkling little laugh.

Elizabeth ignored the mocking tone in Miss Bingley's voice as she emphasised Elizabeth's unmarried status and the meagre size of her house. It was tempting to bite back with a cutting remark, but Elizabeth resisted the urge. She resolved to stay pleasant to all three ladies, for Jane's sake.

Miss Carrington curtseyed, and gave a weak smile.

The poor thing looked miserable. Elizabeth noted her trembling hands and felt sorry for her. She could only have been around twenty-three or twenty-four, yet she carried a weariness much older than her years. Her mousy-brown hair and watery-blue eyes gave her a washed-out look, like old linen which had faded in sunlight.

Mrs. Hurst took up the story. "Our fathers met at school, and were firm friends all their lives. We grew up almost as sisters, did we not Jemima?"

Elizabeth found this surprising, as she had never heard Miss Carrington's name mentioned before by her sisters-in-law. However, she said nothing to contradict Mrs. Hurst.

"And how is Mr. Hurst?" Elizabeth said to his wife, when the conversation paused.

"Oh, Mr. Hurst is away again, for at least a few more days. I shall just have to soldier on without him. Shan't I, dear?" She smiled at Miss Bingley.

"Indeed you shall, sister." They both looked perfectly content with the situation. Elizabeth wondered if they might not actually prefer it this way.

At that moment, Jane appeared in the hallway too, her arms full of mistletoe sprigs. She smiled when she saw Elizabeth, and then stopped suddenly in the middle of the floor when she spotted her sisters-in-law. It seemed that their arrival had come as a surprise to Jane too.

CHAPTER 3

With haste, Jane handed her armful of greenery to a footman. He removed it at once.

"Good afternoon, Mrs. Hurst. Good afternoon Miss Bingley." Jane cleared her throat and curtseyed to her sisters-in-law. "Please forgive my unkempt appearance. I was gathering greenery for the ballroom, and I did not know we would have the pleasure of your company today."

Miss Bingley's smile was fixed and artificial. "Did Charles not tell you we were coming? Silly man. You'd think he'd have had the decency to tell you."

"Yes," agreed Mrs. Hurst. "What *was* he thinking?"

Elizabeth wondered if Miss Bingley or Mrs. Hurst had really told their brother of their intentions. She did not like to think ill of anyone without proof, but she rather suspected they had made the journey without notice to anyone. But that was impossible to verify.

Regardless of the facts of the matter, Miss Bingley was obviously determined to blame Mr. Bingley for the lack of communication. Nobody could contradict her without insulting her. Elizabeth knew Jane would take the information at face value. She never seemed to spot it when people were stretching the truth.

Jane faltered. "Mr. Bingley has been very busy this morning. I expect he—"

"We have brought a friend with us too," Miss Bingley said hurriedly, as though her sister-in-law had not spoken. "Mrs. Bingley, please allow me to present Miss Carrington."

Among the curtseys and greetings, Mrs. Hurst looked around with a faintly appalled expression. "I do hope we are not going to get in the way, my dear Mrs. Bingley. I can see you are rather in chaos."

Jane's face froze in a strained smile, but her

manners were impeccable as she greeted her third unexpected houseguest.

"Delighted, I'm sure. How do you do, Miss Carrington? The more, the merrier. I shall have the guest rooms made up for you all."

"No need," Miss Bingley said, with a smooth wave of her hand. "I caught your steward Grindle on the way downstairs a few moments ago, and gave the order. He said he'd send the chambermaids up immediately."

Jane tolerated this presumption as well as Miss Bingley's interruptions. She was the most even-tempered person in Hertfordshire, Elizabeth felt certain.

But Elizabeth bristled on her behalf. Miss Bingley had no right to order around Jane's servants. It was typical of her to overstep the mark like this.

Miss Bingley looked languidly around the room. "What time will we dine? I do hope we haven't missed dinner." She turned to Mrs. Hurst. "They eat meals so infernally early in the country, do they not?"

Mrs. Hurst nodded, her face taking on a disdainful expression. "Extraordinarily early, sister."

Miss Carrington, while less polished than Mr. Bingley's sisters, had the look of a well-bred girl from a good background. Elizabeth thought she looked kinder than her friends.

"What a pity you did not have better weather for your first journey to Netherfield, Miss Carrington," Elizabeth began.

Before Miss Carrington could respond, Mrs. Hurst cut in. "On the contrary, it was a clement day in London, Miss Bennet. It is much colder out here in Hertfordshire. It always feels colder, when one finds oneself in the middle of nowhere."

"Yes, I agree entirely." Miss Bingley looked around with a pinched expression. "We were warmly-wrapped in our travelling-cloaks, but the temperature had dropped noticeably by the time we reached Finchley. We set off at a most uncivilised hour, you see. It takes so long to get anywhere once you leave the reliable roads of London."

To Elizabeth's relief, they were now led into the drawing room by a harassed-looking servant, promising them refreshments. Elizabeth was glad of the opportunity to stop listening to Miss Bingley's views for a moment.

Jane sidled up to Elizabeth as the other women settled themselves into chairs. They hung back together.

"I do apologise, Lizzy. I shall not have much opportunity to discuss the details of the ball with you in private after all. It seems likely that Mr. Bingley's sisters will wish to involve themselves in the arrangements, now that they are here."

"Very likely." Elizabeth smiled sympathetically at her sister, who now looked quite nervous. "Do not worry, Jane. I shall stay for dinner, and then make my excuses and leave. Too many cooks spoil the broth, after all, and my contributions cannot compare with those of Mrs. Hurst and Miss Bingley. It goes without saying that they have both been to countless high society balls. They will have a great deal of knowledge of the most fashionable way to do things."

"I wish you would stay a while longer," Jane said, clutching her sister's hand. "Conversation always flows more smoothly when you are in a room, Lizzy. You have quite the gift for social interaction. I do envy you that."

Elizabeth laughed. "You flatter me, Jane. I have no such gift. But very well. Then perhaps I shall stay until evening, if that suits you? Mary and Kitty promised me that they would send our father back to bed in a few hours, so I suppose I do not need to hurry back. Not unless a Longbourn footman arrives to tell me I must."

Jane opened her mouth to reply, but there was a squeal from the centre of the room, and a shout of "Charles!" Mr. Bingley had appeared in the doorway.

"Well, well. Here's where you're all hiding," he said, as he crossed the floor. He greeted the assembled company, with the same easy smile and quiet charm that had drawn Jane's eye on their first meeting.

Elizabeth noted the warmth that flowed between the married couple when they greeted one another. That they truly loved and cared for one another was obvious. It made Elizabeth's heart soar to know that her favourite sister had entered into such a loving marriage. There could be no higher goal for a young woman.

"Did you not tell your wife of our intention to arrive today?" Miss Bingley wagged her finger at her brother. "I wrote to you at Christmastide. Did you forget?"

"I received no letter from you, my dear

24

sister," he replied, with a frown. "The last I knew of your intentions, you were to spend the whole of Christmastide in London. I cannot think what happened to your letter." He shook his head in bafflement. "But no matter! You are here now, and our revelries shall be all the better for it."

Elizabeth and Jane exchanged looks. It *was* rather strange to think that a letter from Miss Bingley to Mr. Bingley had gone astray. Their servants were unlikely to lose such correspondence. Far more likely that it had never been sent, thought Elizabeth.

It even occurred to her to wonder if Miss Bingley had engineered the mistake so that she, Mrs. Hurst and Miss Carrington would arrive without warning. That way, Jane would be taken by surprise and bewildered, making her look less competent as a hostess. It was no secret that Miss Bingley had wanted another young lady to marry her brother, and had tried to talk Mr. Bingley out of courting Jane. It was also no secret that Miss Bingley did not respond well to those who thwarted her wishes. She had done this kind of thing before.

Though she did not utter a word of her suspicions, Elizabeth was certain that the lost letter was no accident.

"Let us hear all about your plans for the ball, Mrs. Bingley," Mrs. Hurst ventured. "You must have an evening of festive delight in store for us, I'm sure."

"Well," began Jane, "let me see. We shall of course have a Twelfth Cake. And music. And charades. There shall be a feast at midnight, and we shall dance to the finest orchestra—"

Mrs. Hurst and Miss Bingley looked distinctly underwhelmed. Jane trailed off, looking at each of them in turn.

"Is that all, Mrs. Bingley?" said Miss Bingley. "Do you not mean to have masked revelries? Or to cast lots at the door to decide which gentleman each lady shall be allocated to for the evening?"

Mrs. Hurst looked pityingly at Jane, and nodded. "There really must be something more substantial to do, my dear. Something more exciting, and dangerous. It is Twelfth Night! This is not an everyday ball. Spectacle is vital."

Jane looked stung by their criticisms. Mr. Bingley took his wife's hand and kissed it.

"Now, ladies. This is all a debate over nothing. The ball will be a roaring success, whether it be packed with the sorts of activities you suggest, or not. Fine food, dancing, and good company is all we need to make the night a success. Who could ask for more?"

"*Everyone* asks for more, Charles. It is Twelfth Night!" Mrs. Hurst repeated. "You know as well as we do that your guests will expect something more sophisticated. You are Charles Bingley, not a lowly village squire. Your first ball as a married man is important. Its success will be a mark of your quality."

Jane blushed, as she so frequently did. Elizabeth's heart ached to see her embarrassed by her sisters-in-law.

"I am perhaps not aware of the latest London customs," Jane said, at last. "Do tell me more, so that I might modify the details of our plan accordingly."

Mrs. Hurst began to list her ideas for an appropriate Twelfth Night Ball, while Miss Bingley added observations and opinions at intervals. Their friend Miss Carrington remained mute, just as she had from the moment Elizabeth arrived. To the silent girl's credit, Elizabeth noticed that Miss Carrington seemed uncomfortable with her friends' conduct. Elizabeth caught the quiet girl's eye and smiled reassuringly.

Before long, Jane had more suggestions than she knew what to do with, and the servants were summoning them all to dinner.

AFTER A SUMPTUOUS MEAL — which impressed Elizabeth, who was only too aware that at least four of the guests had arrived unannounced— the ladies retired. Mr. Bingley, as the sole gentleman, made his way alone to the library to discuss a few matters with his steward.

Jane took Elizabeth's arm as they walked back to the drawing room.

"Oh, Lizzy. I am ill-suited to this task. Perhaps it would have been better if I had asked my sisters-in-law to help me earlier! Will we even have time to prepare all the games and novelties required for a smart Twelfth Night ball?"

"Jane, you need not worry. This is Hertfordshire, not Mayfair. We are easily pleased. I am sure most of your guests will have no awareness of any brand-new London customs. And anyone who enjoys the ball less because of a lack of complex diversions must be quite determined not to have fun. Please steady your self-doubt. You are doing a marvellous job as the lady of the house, and you need not worry."

"I thank you, Lizzy. You always have a way of putting me at ease."

"What else are sisters for?" Elizabeth kissed her sister's cheek and took her arm.

Jane and Elizabeth joined the other three ladies in the drawing room, and closed the door.

Mrs. Hurst sat down to play an air on the pianoforte, and they all listened politely. Her technical skill as a player was astounding. But there was a coldness in her perfection which rather ruined the experience for Elizabeth. It was as though she was passionless, and merely well-rehearsed. Her music was a great deal more listenable than that of Mary Bennet, however, and for this small mercy Elizabeth was grateful.

Miss Carrington still had not said a word all evening beyond her initial greetings, and the appropriate use of "please" and "thank you" at the dinner table. The poor girl could not get a word in edgewise when Miss Bingley was at the table. Elizabeth decided to try again to engage her in conversation.

"Have you been to a Twelfth Night ball before, Miss Carrington?"

Miss Carrington looked startled, as though surprised anyone would address her directly. Then she spoke. "Yes, I have attended a few. I have been out since I was sixteen. My family always attends a number of balls at Christmas-tide, in Lincolnshire."

"That must be very enjoyable. How old are you now?"

"Twenty-two. I was—" She stopped suddenly in the middle of the sentence.

While waiting for her to complete her thoughts, Elizabeth noticed that Miss Carrington's attention had suddenly been stolen. Elizabeth turned to see what was distracting her companion. It seemed that her eyes were focused on something happening on the other side of the window.

A carriage had pulled into the driveway of Netherfield. Elizabeth could not see the entire scene from her vantage point, but she saw enough to make out that it was a fine carriage, pulled by four elegant horses.

"Mr. Darcy is here!" exclaimed Miss Bingley.

Miss Carrington's face showed no signs of recognising the name, but when she saw her friends' response, she looked as interested as anyone.

Jane caught Elizabeth's eye and raised her eyebrows at her. Elizabeth raised hers in return, amused. Apparently Mr. Darcy's arrival was quite an event.

They did not have to wait long for the man himself to come in. Within a few minutes, the double doors opened. Elizabeth turned towards them, and the four other ladies did the same.

Mr. Bingley came bounding into the room, with a grin on his face. He was accompanied by a tall, dark-haired gentleman, and a blonde, slight young lady.

"Look who's here!" Mr. Bingley exclaimed.

"Oh, goodness!" Miss Bingley said, looking unusually flustered.

"Mr. Darcy and Miss Darcy," announced the footman.

CHAPTER 4

D arcy gave his sister Georgiana a slight nod, to reassure her. She was nervous in the company of strangers these days. That was hardly surprising, given her recent unfortunate experience.

He patted her hand, threaded into the crook of his elbow. She smiled, looking up at him with what he knew was a measure of brave resolve.

The footman opened the door and announced them. Bingley introduced them all, with his customary sunshine-infused manner, and made the required perfunctory remarks. Darcy greeted his friend's new wife, who seemed charming and demure. Bingley's sisters babbled some nonsense or other, as they usually did.

Darcy barely listened to any of it, because he had suddenly been struck by lightning.

He had not been literally struck by anything at all, of course, but certainly it was as though a bolt from heaven had rendered him speechless for a moment.

Before him, a pair of uncommonly lively dark eyes glittered at him, framed by a fair young female face. Arguably, her looks were only a little more favourable than average, and she wore no greatly fashionable attire to draw the eye. Yet, in a roomful of people, he saw only her.

He recovered his manners quickly. "Miss Bingley. Mrs. Hurst. You remember my sister, of course: Miss Darcy."

"Of course." Mrs. Hurst extended an elegant hand and took Georgiana's in hers. "Such a pretty little thing. Do come in, dear. We are just about to enjoy some more music."

Georgiana blushed to the tips of her ears, and reluctantly allowed herself to be drawn into the room. Darcy caught his friend's eye, and spoke quietly, for his ears only.

"Bingley, is that dark-haired girl your sister-in-law?"

"Miss Bennet? Why, yes." Bingley suddenly

looked delighted, and beamed at his friend. "Gracious, Darcy. Have you taken an instant fancy to the young lady?"

Darcy shook his head. He was not in the habit of sharing his private thoughts, for one thing. He never had, and he was sure he never would.

"Not in the least. Don't be ridiculous."

"Come now, Darcy. It would be no great hardship to find yourself a bride. You cannot rattle around in that vast estate all by yourself."

Darcy gave an impatient frown. "I do not live by myself. I have Georgiana to look after."

"A wife brings a whole new level of fulfilment to life. Believe me, Darcy. I know." He looked over at Mrs. Bingley, a look of pure joy on his face.

Darcy sighed sharply. "I have no desire for a bride, Bingley. We have settled this matter before. Please set the subject aside."

"As you wish, my friend. I shall not play matchmaker, be assured. But mark my words! I shall see you married off one of these days. You shall change your mind when you meet the right lady."

Bingley's laugh was as light-hearted and

affectionate as ever. As such, Darcy could not possibly be irritated by him.

He sometimes wondered what it would be like to be such an open, amiable character as his friend. It was so far outside Darcy's scope of experience, he could scarcely imagine it.

He certainly did not wish to marry, though. That was plain truth. Attachments to others were only an encumbrance, and he could do without any of those. It was too much trouble to form relationships with people, only to lose them at some point, or perhaps to leave them bereft. As he had experienced with his beloved parents at a young age, people he loved could be snatched away without a moment's notice. Life was hard enough without adding grief and torment into the bargain.

Besides, he did not wish to be accountable to another. He would take care of Georgiana to the end of his days, and had arranged to leave a good sum for provision of her care if he were to leave the earth before her. Other than that, he wished no more responsibility than the ownership of his Derbyshire estate and his horses. That was quite enough for him.

"Come, Mr. Darcy. Do join us around the

pianoforte. My sister has sheet music for a new sonata, and it is awfully melodious. I am sure you will find it to your taste." Mrs. Hurst smiled sweetly at Darcy. He scowled.

"Oh yes, what a good idea," Bingley said, patting Darcy on the back. "Look, Miss Darcy is already sitting comfortably beside the pianoforte, with Miss Carrington. We should join them."

Darcy once again caught the eye of Miss Bennet. He felt a warmth flicker through him, which quickly dissipated when she looked away. It was quite an extraordinary sensation. For some reason, he found he did not want it to end. Without examining what the feeling meant, he simply followed his instincts and approached her. Mr. Bingley had already introduced them, so he was able to start a conversation.

Darcy waited for his friend to sit beside his wife before speaking to the bewitching stranger.

"Do you play, Miss Bennet?"

She looked up, apparently startled. Their eyes locked together for a few seconds too long, before she broke the spell by looking down at her hands, folded in her lap. When she raised her face to him again, she was fully composed.

"Yes, Mr. Darcy. I very much enjoy playing the pianoforte at home with my sisters."

"Then perhaps we might hear your favourite piece later."

"Thank you, but no. I have no longing to entertain others."

"Ah, you are modest. That is an admirable quality in a lady. Nevertheless, I hope we may prevail on you before the afternoon is over."

His eyes drank in the sight of her, as she sat demurely. Her dark curls framed her heart-shaped face most becomingly, and the curve of her small rosebud mouth when she smiled at him was pleasing. Sadly, her smile was all too fleeting.

"Really, sir. I beg to be excused. Mrs. Hurst seems eager to enrich us with her gifts, and I am content to sit back and let her do so."

A lady who did not court attention? He could not remember having ever come across such a rare creature. The ladies he mixed with in London — and in Derbyshire, come to that — spent a good deal of time and energy trying to win favour with dancing, singing, playing, and various other accomplishments. Yet here was one actively avoiding the gaze of the room.

He searched for another topic of conversation. "You mentioned that you and Mrs. Bingley have other sisters. And are they out?"

"Yes sir, we have three more sisters. They are all out. At least two will attend the ball on Friday." A slight tension danced across her forehead. Quickly, she smiled, and the tension disappeared. "My mother will be there also."

"And your father?"

"Regrettably, my father will probably be confined to the house. He is unwell at present."

"I am sorry to hear it."

Miss Bennet nodded and smiled. "Thank you."

As Mrs. Hurst began to play, their conversation naturally stopped so that they might listen. The room filled with music. Mrs. Hurst's playing was undoubtedly excellent, but Darcy's attention was still elsewhere. He made a good show of listening to the sonata, while keeping half an eye on the young lady with the twinkling eyes.

Miss Bingley sidled over to them both with a coquettish look. "Well, Mr. Darcy. Is not my sister quite the most marvellous pianist you have ever heard?"

She fluttered her eyelashes as she said this.

Darcy supposed she had something in her eye, and ignored it politely.

"I am afraid not. There are a great many pianists in London of exceptional proficiency. I could not rank your sister among them."

Miss Bingley seemed to be thrown off-course a little by this response. She gave a little high-pitched laugh, and moved slightly closer to Darcy, so the sides of their arms were almost touching.

"Oh, but Miss Bennet! *You* will agree with me, I am sure. Do you not find Mrs. Hurst's playing remarkable?"

Miss Bennet looked up. She glanced at Darcy, and over to Mrs. Hurst, with a reluctant expression. "I regret that I am no great judge of quality, Miss Bingley. But I find Mrs. Hurst's playing very enjoyable."

That was a good answer, Darcy thought. *She has a more diplomatic turn of phrase than I.* As someone who prided himself on his ability to delineate a thought neatly, this came as some surprise.

"Well, we are all very accomplished, in our family." Miss Bingley lifted her head so she was almost looking down her nose at Miss Bennet.

"Our brother has a number of talents too, of course."

"Indeed," Darcy agreed. "He is the finest horseman in the county, and has more patience than any man I know."

"Virtues indeed," said Miss Bennet. She offered her rosebud smile to him first, before offering a weaker version to Miss Bingley. His heart jolted.

Disconcerted at his own reaction to Miss Bennet, he bowed at her stiffly. He had to move away from her, before he said or did something to betray his instant attraction to her.

Fortunately, at that moment, Mrs. Hurst reached the end of the first sheet of notation, and Miss Carrington had trouble turning it over. Mrs. Bingley then stood and moved to the pianoforte to assist her sister-in-law.

Seeing that Bingley's ear was now available, Darcy excused himself from Miss Bennet and Miss Bingley with a bow, and hastened towards his old friend.

"Enjoying yourself, Darcy?" Bingley asked, with a grin. "Caroline has been looking forward to seeing you again. She could speak of nothing else when I last saw her."

Mr. Darcy looked out of the window, uncomfortable at the idea of Miss Bingley being quite so keen to see him.

"Georgiana needs to buy sundries while we are at Netherfield," he said, briskly changing the subject. "I propose to take her into Meryton tomorrow, to visit the various establishments there. Would you and Mrs. Bingley care to join us?"

"Regrettably, I am not at liberty to join you tomorrow, Darcy. Mrs. Bingley has a morning of ball preparation scheduled with the steward and servants, and I promised my sisters I would accompany them on a tour of Netherfield with Miss Carrington."

"And it will take you all morning to walk around your estate with three ladies?"

"No, but it will not leave enough time to travel into Meryton as well. Besides, I have some estate business to deal with too. Perhaps we might reconvene later in the afternoon?"

"Of course." The matter was thus closed, and Mr. Darcy prepared himself for a morning of shopping with his sister. His heart sank a little. Georgiana was not an extravagant girl, and he had no concerns about her spending, but she was indecisive. It could take her all morning to choose the ribbon for a single bonnet. He had rather hoped for the kindly guiding hand of a sensible lady, which he had imagined Mrs. Bingley could provide. There was nothing to be done, however, so he would make the best of it.

Mrs. Hurst's sonata came to an end and they all clapped politely. Mr. Darcy joined in, though he had not really been listening.

"Oh, do let us have another!" cried Miss Bingley. After the required protestations, and false refusals, Mrs. Hurst sat down once more at the instrument.

Georgiana appeared happy, and Miss Carrington still sat next to her, giving every impression of having made a new friend. Darcy was glad about that.

Reassured, Darcy strolled a few feet away to look out of the window, and observed a few stray flakes of snow fluttering down from the heavens. The sky was a marbled white, looking every inch a perfect English winter sky.

He hoped the winter would bring Georgiana more peace of mind than the summer had.

"We shall have refreshments within the hour," Mr. Bingley announced, as Mrs. Hurst's opening bars rang out across the room. After one more surreptitious glance at Miss Bennet, Darcy settled down in a chair, pretending to listen to the music, while his mind wandered all over England. Had he examined his thoughts more closely, he might have noticed that a certain dark-eyed young lady was hovering among them all.

CHAPTER 5

Elizabeth observed the party, as Mrs. Hurst played a second piece on the pianoforte. Elizabeth did not recognise the tune, though it was perhaps better known in the higher echelons of society. Miss Bingley and Miss Carrington certainly seemed to recognise it, for they exclaimed joyfully when it began.

The new people Elizabeth had met were most intriguing. Mr. Darcy was an imposing, tall man, with a fine figure, a well-aspected face, and a determined jaw. He stood proudly, as though he were looking down on the sitting company, both figuratively and literally. Elizabeth had the feeling he was rarely very much impressed by anything.

His sister, Miss Darcy, by contrast, was a delicate blonde young lady, with wide eyes and a sweet expression. Truly, she had the makings of a great beauty, though she was yet too young to have fully grown into her looks. She could not have been more than sixteen, Elizabeth guessed. As Miss Darcy smiled shyly at them all, the warmth of her smile lit up her whole face most becomingly.

On first introduction, Elizabeth felt for some reason that she had somehow caught Mr. Darcy's attention for longer than the others. His serious eyes burned into her for a moment. The depth of his stare threw her off-kilter for a moment. When she met his gaze with her own, he bowed. She curtseyed, then averted her own gaze.

Her first impression was that Mr. Darcy was just the sort of gentleman she preferred to avoid. Full of superiority, his disinterested glances around the room made it clear he felt himself far too good for anything or anyone in it. Elizabeth did not have patience for such a man today. She was too concerned about her father, and about Lydia, to find the energy to converse with a cold, haughty, proud person such as he.

Mr. Bingley undertook the task of making introductions around the room. "Mr. Darcy, may

I present my wonderful wife? We are very happy together." They smiled at one another, and Elizabeth could not help but smile along with them. "This happiness is now made all the deeper by my being able to share it with you, my friend."

Mr. Darcy bowed. "Congratulations on the joyful occasion of your matrimony. I must offer my sincerest apologies to you both for missing your wedding. As Mr. Bingley knows, Miss Darcy and I were unavoidably detained elsewhere, Mrs. Bingley. Not for all the world would I have wished to miss your wedding."

"Do not give it another thought, dear fellow," laughed Mr. Bingley, clapping his old friend on the back. "You are excused without any complaint. I know you would have been there if you could."

Jane smiled warmly as Mr. Darcy took her hand and bowed once more. "You were missed, Mr. Darcy, but we quite understood. Thank you for bestowing on us the honour of your visit now."

Suitably introduced, the company resumed the afternoon's activities. The only difference was the addition of two new people. Now they were here, the afternoon's activities were split between teasing out the finer details of the forth-coming Netherfield ball, and quizzing the taci-turn Mr. Darcy. Needless to say, Miss Bingley and Mrs. Hurst took the lead on both fronts.

"Oh, Mr. Darcy, you must tell us all about your adventures." Mrs. Hurst's eyes gleamed. "You were very mysterious earlier, you know. We need the whole story, from start to finish."

Mr. Darcy's mouth was set firmly, and he seemed only superficially engaged in the conver-sation. "I shall not bore you all with an account of our activities these last months."

"Come now, Mr. Darcy. You really must indulge our curiosity. What can have been so diverting that you missed your dear friend's wedding?"

"As I said, Mrs. Hurst, it would be of no interest to you."

Mrs. Hurst and Miss Bingley looked taken aback. But there was nothing to be done. Eliza-beth knew they could not persist further without seeming rude. So they laughed their chiming-bell laughs, and their conversation moved elsewhere.

Elizabeth entertained herself by scrutinising each guest whenever one of them turned away, or became embroiled in conversation. People-watching was by far her favourite sport. The present company provided many interesting targets for her.

She noted that Miss Carrington said almost nothing in company. The young lady was evidently from a family of good means, but seemed to lack the confidence and self-assurance usually found in well-educated girls. Elizabeth was intrigued by this mismatch, and decided she would try to engage Miss Carrington in further conversation later.

Mrs. Hurst and Miss Bingley were sociable and observed etiquette perfectly, but Elizabeth always felt that a streak of something rather like spite ran through them both. She found it difficult to understand why they had befriended Miss Carrington in particular. Miss Carrington did not seem the sort of person Elizabeth imagined they would seek out as a friend. Surely they preferred outgoing fashionable types like themselves? Furthermore, why had they brought Miss Carrington to Netherfield with them to celebrate Twelfth Night?

Elizabeth had not the faintest idea why Miss Carrington had been taken under their wings, but supposed she would find out in due course. At any rate, she lacked the capacity to guess.

Mr. Darcy was another mystery. To all who engaged him in conversation, he seemed to respond perfectly in accordance with prevailing standards of politeness. No technical fault could be found in his manners, nor in his attentiveness to the company. Perhaps he was a little abrupt in some of his answers, but he broke no social law.

However, underneath that well-bred exterior, Elizabeth sensed something else. Detachment? Boredom? Perhaps also distraction by something more interesting? There was an impatience in his face that spoke volumes. Instinctively, she felt Mr. Darcy had already grown tired of their humdrum chatter, and would seize any opportunity to do something else instead.

She knew sweet Jane would see only gentlemanly conduct in her new guest. But Elizabeth knew better.

When Mr. Darcy was not being spoken to, he made it very obvious through his lack of interest that he would rather be elsewhere.

Elizabeth detected more than just a man frustrated at the low calibre of social exchange. He showed the usual disinterest of the upper classes in those they considered their inferiors, and the frustration of the quick mind being forced to slow down for more plodding conversation. It was written all over his face. They bored him, and he could not hide it.

No, Mr. Darcy did not break social rules, but he clearly had contempt for them. While he kept to the letter of the social law, he was very far from following the spirit of it.

Elizabeth had encountered this tendency before, upon meeting her cousin Mr. Collins's patron. Lady Catherine de Bourgh had made it very plain how much lower down the social scale she considered the Bennets. Elizabeth had found the whole visit most disagreeable.

That same feeling of social injustice rose again in Elizabeth, as she observed Mr. Darcy's supercilious behaviour.

Her sister's words yesterday came back to her too. Jane had casually suggested that Mr. Darcy might be a good match for Elizabeth. Ridiculous! The longer they spent in the same room, the more Elizabeth could see that a match between them would never be possible, not even if Elizabeth had ten thousand pounds a year and a house in Mayfair. Mr. Darcy's demeanour alone was enough to convince her of his unsuitability. The very idea was laughable. Even Jane must agree, now she had met him.

Elizabeth was certain that if she ever got to know Mr. Darcy, she would discover his true personality was the cold haughtiness of the very rich. It was not a demeanour that had ever impressed Elizabeth, nor ever would.

But this would not do. She could not sit here analysing personalities all afternoon. It may be enjoyable, but she ought to engage with the company, not sit apart from them. Otherwise, she was no better than Mr. Darcy herself.

Elizabeth forced herself to concentrate on Mrs. Hurst's soaring pianoforte crescendo. She had only to stay in the company of Mr. Darcy, Miss Bingley and Mrs. Hurst until evening. She could manage that, at least.

AFTER MRS. HURST'S second sonata, the conversation lulled. Before she noticed what was happening, Elizabeth suddenly found herself adjacent to Mr. Darcy. They had exchanged some trivial words earlier, but here they were again. Conversation was a necessity.

"I wonder why you did not choose to spend Twelfth Night in London, Mr. Darcy?" she began.

"I missed my friend's wedding," he said, simply. "I am here to make amends."

The response did not surprise her. Mr. Darcy had come to Netherfield to discharge a debt, and not for his own merriment. Of course he had. What enjoyment could he find here in the Hertfordshire countryside?

"I trust you will not find us country folk too tedious while you are here," she said. "We have such plain tastes, and such simple ways, that we must contrast most unfavourably with your usual company."

"Not at all. Country folk are much the same as town folk. One drawing room conversation is much like another."

"You think so?"

"By and large, they are all fairly tedious." His gaze held hers, unyielding. "Very occasionally, one finds oneself engaged in a conversation which is not wholly deficient in merit."

His eyes flashed at her and she heard her own

pulse throbbing in her ears. What an infernally rude man.

"I disagree, Mr. Darcy. Surely *all* drawing room conversations are edifying? Every one of them teaches us more about one another than we realise."

"Indeed?" He cast an eye over Mr. Bingley's sisters, who had begun to argue with one another about something trivial. "I find most teach us nothing we did not already know."

"You do not believe confirmation of one's suspicions is, in itself, useful?"

The corner of his mouth twitched, as though he was suppressing a smile. But no smile broke through.

"On the contrary, Miss Bennet. Some conversations are simply a monumental waste of time." He glanced across the room once more, then fixed her with his eyes again. "I daresay the trick lies in identifying which is which. Then one might allocate one's time accordingly."

"Are you quick to dismiss those whose conversation displeases you?"

"Not in the least, Miss Bennet." His eyes gleamed at her. "Are you?"

Elizabeth opened her mouth to reply, but

could not think of a single thing to say all of a sudden. All she knew was that she felt uncomfortable, and she did not wish the feeling to persist.

This was too much. She had enough in life to think about, without entering into a circular debate with an arrogant stranger in her leisure time.

Before he could speak again, she stood up.

"Forgive me, Mr. Darcy. I need to leave Netherfield soon, and I have just remembered that I must consult with my sister before I leave. Would you please excuse me?"

With an imploring look to Jane, she curtseyed to Mr. Darcy. Jane, receptive as always to her sister's needs, stood immediately and made her way to the door.

Mr. Darcy bowed, looking confounded, and stood back as Elizabeth swept past him. He was still watching her when she walked to Jane, but he said nothing more.

CHAPTER 6

"**D**o you need me further, Jane?"

Elizabeth clasped her hands together in front of her. She was vexed to notice they were trembling slightly.

Jane looked at her sister with a puzzled expression. "What do you mean? Is there something wrong, Lizzy?"

"No, nothing is wrong. I fear I am no match for your fine London friends, that is all. I fancy I will leave you all to get on with the business of planning."

"Why do you say that, dear sister? Has somebody offended you?"

Elizabeth could scarcely explain how she felt. All she knew was that she was experiencing a visceral reaction to the gentleman to whom she had just spoken. She had no idea why, other than the fact that his conceited, snobbish manner irritated her. Yet would that usually be enough to send her into such a spin? She was not so sure.

"Forgive me, Jane. I have not slept well this week, and I am worried about our parents and Lydia. I fear it is affecting my judgment, and my social interactions, and I do not wish to behave in an unbecoming manner. The last thing I would ever want to do is to embarrass you, as your sister."

"Gracious, Lizzy! That is not possible. I am always proud to call you my sister."

"If you will excuse me, it is best that I make my way back to Longbourn now. You need no help from me with the ball, as you have such experienced assistants here." Elizabeth knew she was talking too quickly, yet could not slow herself. "The ball shall be a magnificent event, whatever form it takes. You have already hired musicians, let us remember. Mrs. Hurst will be sure to supplement their arts with those of her own. And your cook is marvellous, and quite the best purveyor of white soup I have ever known. And the entire occasion will be the talk of the county. That much is certain. And—"

Elizabeth was falling over her own words now. Jane looked at her curiously.

"Are you feeling quite well, Lizzy?"

"Yes. Goodness, yes. Very well, thank you. Would you send for my maid? She can let the coachman know we will soon be leaving."

Jane agreed, but still looked somewhat perturbed. She sent a footman to fetch Elizabeth's maid and prepare the travelling-cloaks.

The remaining party was now embroiled in a lively conversation, and Elizabeth did not wish to interrupt to take her leave yet. She sat down in an armchair beside the door, and picked up a book, awaiting notification of her maid's readiness.

Before she could find another reason to escape, Mr. Darcy had made his way over to her once more. He did not sit in the chair next to hers, but instead towered over her, tall as an oak.

Elizabeth was aware of five pairs of female eyes suddenly alighting on them both from across the room.

"I do hope I have not said anything to prompt your sudden decision to leave, Miss Bennet."

"Of course not." Elizabeth held his eye contact defiantly, though she felt the odd sensation of butterflies fluttering through her abdomen. "What an absurd notion. Please allow me to reassure you, sir. I merely have duties to attend to."

"Perhaps it is just that the conversation was too tedious for you, Miss Bennet?"

"Not in the least, Mr. Darcy." She lifted her chin a little higher. "One drawing room conversation is quite like another, after all. And our exchange was not wholly deficient in merit."

She thought she detected a little flash of something in his dark eyes. Amusement? No. The man did not seem to be the humorous type.

"I am glad to hear it."

"In truth, sir, I must return home to attend to our father. He is not well, as I mentioned earlier."

Mr. Darcy's face became grave once more. The twinkle in his eye was gone. He bowed. "An admirable inclination, Miss Bennet. I do hope you find your father much improved."

"Thank you."

"Before I take my leave of you, I must ask one thing. May I be the first to have the honour of dancing with you at the ball on Friday?"

Elizabeth was quite taken aback. Had Mr.

Darcy really just requested the first dance at the Twelfth Night, two days in advance?

Had he really asked *her*, of all the fine ladies he could have approached?

Why?

She could not unravel his reasoning. More pertinently, she could not refuse either, without finding herself forced to sit out all the dances. Indeed, she had no choice but to accept, if she wished to dance at the ball at all.

Did she really wish to spend the first half-hour of the ball in the company of a proud, unsmiling man, who felt he was better than everybody else in the room? Not a bit of it. But that was the situation in which she found herself.

Once more, his solemn dark gaze set off a flutter of disquiet inside Elizabeth. She disliked the feeling intensely. She could only conclude that she intensely disliked Mr. Darcy.

Staring back at him, she found herself speechless. She was unable to refuse, but also unwilling to accept.

It was imperative that she answer promptly now, but she could hardly bring herself to give in to him.

Fortunately, her maid appeared at that very moment.

"I offer more apologies, but I really must leave now," she said, standing up. She turned to the rest of the company. They were still all staring in her direction. "It was a pleasure to see you again, Mrs. Hurst and Miss Bingley. And I am very glad to make your acquaintance, Miss Darcy and Mr. Darcy, and Miss Carrington. I do hope you enjoy your stay at Netherfield." She curtseyed deeply to the company as one.

"You did not reply to my question, Miss Bennet," Mr. Darcy said, in his deep aristocratic voice. "Therefore I shall take your silence as acceptance."

Elizabeth's cheeks felt hot. The nerve of the man.

He knew she had to accept. He knew she was his for the first dances, whether she liked it or not.

"Then I believe I shall see you at the ball, Mr Darcy," she said dryly, and marched out of the room.

CHAPTER 7

Elizabeth spent the journey home in a state of mental turbulence. Her mind wandered over the events of the afternoon, from Miss Bingley's barbed comments, to Mr. Darcy's haughty manner, to the moment when he had amazed her by asking her to dance so far in advance of the ball.

Not for the first time, she reflected irritably on the social rules between men and women. It is intolerable to be compelled to dance with one man, or dance with no man at all, she complained to herself. *Why must we women endure such restrictions?*

The coach jolted over a stony path. Elizabeth had to hold onto the side to avoid slipping off the seat. She sighed sharply, and peered out of the window, even though it was now dark. Twilight always arrived early in January, and the cold night air whistled in through the gaps in the carriage. She pulled her cloak more tightly around herself.

It pained her to note the way that Mr. Darcy's arrival had caused an uncommon agitation in her. But why had it happened at all? Had he really done anything terribly wrong?

She could not put her finger on exactly why she felt so ill-disposed towards him. Her feelings were muddled. She examined them closely as the carriage bumped down the lane.

Had she ever previously experienced an aversion to a man's character, at first encounter? She could not remember a time when that had happened.

A terrible thought crept into her mind.

She cast her thoughts back to the moment Mr. Bingley, Mr. Darcy, and Miss Darcy had walked in the room. The moment Mr. Darcy had looked at her, she had felt a disturbance inside. It had both unsettled and annoyed her. What was the reason for this aversion?

Was it even an aversion?

"Oh, good Lord," she muttered to herself.

Her maid looked up in alarm. "Miss? Is everything all right? Shall I ask the driver to slow down?"

"No, no. The opposite. Ask him to hurry home. I need to get back to Longbourn at once."

The maid climbed up to relay the message to the driver, and Lizzy rested her head on the side of the carriage, though the journey was far too bumpy for her to be comfortable in that position.

Could what she was feeling for Mr. Darcy be... attraction?

It was unthinkable. Surely nobody could be drawn to a man in one respect, and repelled by him in another?

She had taken an interest in other young men previously, of course. As a teenager, she had enjoyed watching the handsome soldiers as they marched through Meryton, and dreamed of one day marrying one.

Once, when visiting her aunt and uncle in London, she had met a man at a ball whom she found very agreeable. He had behaved most charmingly to Elizabeth, and had given her to believe a proposal would soon be forthcoming. Mr. and Mrs. Gardiner had been overjoyed at their niece's good fortune. Not two weeks later, they had discovered he was already promised to another. The rogue's duplicitous behaviour had come as a disappointment, but Elizabeth had felt none of the inner turmoil she did now. She had found the man pleasing company, and attractive to look at, but there had been little more to it than that.

She had no experience of the feeling Mr. Darcy brought out in her. It was all new, and uncomfortable. She did not like it one bit.

What did it mean? Should she avoid Mr. Darcy altogether? She could not miss her sister's first ball as hostess without causing Jane great sorrow. That was unthinkable. No, she had to go. That much was certain.

Moreover, she would have to dance with Mr. Darcy, as promised. There was no way of avoiding it, if she wished to dance at all. He had backed her into a corner on that matter.

But she would avoid him for the rest of the evening. Yes, that would be best. She would throw herself wholeheartedly into the festive merrymaking, and dance as often as possible with as many gentlemen as she could. The more gregarious she was, the less time she would need to spend with Mr. Darcy at all. Perfect.

In addition, Miss Bingley and Mrs. Hurst had suggested that the guests draw lots at the door, to allocate each lady and gentleman to a partner. The odds of any of the Bennets being paired with Mr. Darcy were slim at best. Elizabeth would have the perfect excuse to focus only on her partner for the night, and could not be thought rude for doing so. The source of her discomfort would only be temporarily unavoidable. That was another shred of comfort to cling to.

The ball would finish around six o'clock in the morning, and by then, she would be ready for her carriage home to Longbourn. Furthermore, the very next morning, Mr. Darcy and his sister would head back to London with the Bingleys. Elizabeth's regret at saying goodbye to her sister would be tempered by her relief at seeing Mrs. Hurst, Miss Bingley, and Mr. Darcy leave the neighbourhood. Equilibrium would be restored once more.

Having resolved all this in her own mind, Elizabeth felt rather better. It was going to be all right.

By the time the carriage reached Longbourn, Elizabeth had come to terms completely with her perplexing feelings, and was feeling more relaxed about the ball altogether.

She would support Jane and represent the unmarried women of her family as best she could. Perhaps she might even enjoy herself a little too.

Elizabeth had every expectation that her mother would make a full recovery in time to attend the ball. Equally, she knew her father would not go if he had even the slightest excuse to miss it. He had never enjoyed balls, and would not mind being confined to Longbourn one bit. He would probably rather enjoy the opportunity to read in peace. She did not begrudge him that. Not everybody was the sociable type, after all.

The carriage came to a standstill on the gravel of the driveway and the driver opened her door. Elizabeth's maid jumped out first, then held the door open while the driver helped Elizabeth down.

As Elizabeth slipped off her cloak off and handed it to her maid, Elizabeth heard the distinctive sound of Mary's singing.

"Oh dear," she murmured to herself. "I do hope Mary is not trying to entertain Father."

Peeling off her gloves, she made her way

through to the drawing room to find out.

"I TOLD YOU. He was tired. He didn't want anything to eat."

Elizabeth's frustration grew. She paced the room as she spoke. "But how did he *look*, Kitty? Did he seem more unwell? It is most unlike Father to refuse dinner."

"Oh, keep still, Lizzy," said Mary. "You're giving me a headache, marching up and down like a sentry-guard. Sit down, or at least stand still."

"Hush, Mary. Kitty, please. Think. Did Father's health seem to have deteriorated?"

"I don't know. Perhaps. He did look a little pale."

Elizabeth ran upstairs without another word. She knocked softly at her father's bedchamber door. Not a sound.

"Papa?" she called.

She turned the handle and opened the door. Inside, her father was propped up in bed with a bank of pillows. His nightcap was askew, and he had obviously fallen asleep reading, because the book had slipped to the edge of the eiderdown, and looked likely to crash to the floor at any moment. She eased it from his hands, and replaced it on the bedside table.

"Dear Papa," she whispered, as she straightened his nightcap.

He murmured and turned his head, but remained asleep. His cheeks did look a little more waxen than they had that morning, but he was sleeping soundly, and she saw no reason to wake him. She would send word to the doctor to visit again tomorrow morning.

Anger at her sisters for not sending a footman to Netherfield was mixed with a sense of guilt at having been distracted at all by the matter of the Twelfth Night ball. She had wasted a good stretch of time analysing her own odd reaction to Mr. Darcy too, as though it were of any importance whatsoever. What a trivial concern both matters now seemed.

"I should not have left Longbourn today," she said to herself, as she descended the stairs. She resolved to remain at home until she could be sure her father was well enough to manage without her. If that meant missing the ball, she was sure Jane would understand.

CHAPTER 8

E lizabeth's needlework was unusually irksome that evening. She found her needle slipped frequently, and at one point she stabbed herself in the thumb and drew blood.

"Lizzy! You haven't been this clumsy since you were knee-high to a spider. Is there something wrong?" Kitty could occasionally be perceptive, though she was ordinarily too self-absorbed to apply her skills to others.

"No, there's nothing wrong, Kitty. I am just concerned for our father. But he sleeps soundly, and breathes freely. I hope the doctor will be able to put our minds at rest in the morning."

"Mother will be up at last tomorrow, too," said Mary, abruptly.

Elizabeth gave her a quizzical look. "How do you know that?"

"She said so, when I went to see her this afternoon. She is getting awfully bored alone in her chamber. Nobody to talk to, you see. And you know how Mamma loves to talk."

Elizabeth smiled. "That is quite true." She had guessed her mother could not keep away from talk of Jane's ball, and was amused to hear she had been right.

Mary wagged her book in emphasis. "When the kitchen maid popped in yesterday with a tray of refreshments, Mamma kept the poor girl talking so long, the cook became most impatient. Nothing is getting done downstairs, apparently. Mamma insists on an audience for her grievances, and the steward simply can't spare the staff. So tomorrow she is going to get up and come downstairs to breakfast."

"Oh dear," Kitty said, with a sigh. "Breakfast has been so tranquil these last few days. Mamma will have days' worth of conversation stored up, and will want to air it all immediately. I rather wonder if anything shall be eaten at all."

Elizabeth chuckled. "Oh, I think we'll

manage. It will be nice to return to something approaching normality."

Kitty flapped a hand at Elizabeth. "Never mind all that. How is our dear Jane? Is she happy?" Kitty was always keen to hear stories of her married sister's life, which seemed impossibly glamorous to her. "I cannot wait for the ball. I shall dance all night long, until hours after dawn."

"Be sure to wear sturdy shoes, then. And yes, Jane is very well, thank you. Mr. Bingley is an attentive husband, and Netherfield is a comfortable home. She has risen to a most agreeable situation in life."

"Now we just need to get *you* married off," Kitty giggled. "If it's not too late."

"Well, thank you very much," Elizabeth said, with raised eyebrows. "I like to think it is never too late, if one were to meet the right person."

Mary shook her head. "Oh, Lizzy will never meet anyone. She's far too judgmental."

"Judgmental? Me?" Elizabeth started unpicking a line of her embroidery. She had used the wrong stitch style, for the entire leaf motif. How silly of her. "Why do you say that?"

"Look at the way you reacted to Mrs. Collins's engagement! You were horrified that Mrs. Collins would marry our cousin. You nearly combusted!"

"Oh, Mary. We were all horrified at that, were we not? Charlotte is such a sensible, kind woman, and Mr. Collins is far from anybody's idea of an ideal husband. You were just as astounded as I. Am I wrong?"

Kitty came to Elizabeth's aid. "Lizzy is right, Mary. We all thought Mrs. Collins was temporarily insane to agree to marry Mr. Collins. Still, she seems happy enough."

"So she does." Elizabeth had to concur that Mr. and Mrs. Collins did appear to be content with their lot. It may have had more to do with their habit of never spending much time together than with any innate compatibility. Either way, it could not truthfully be said to be a bad match.

"Did Mr. Bingley bring a handsome friend to Netherfield, by any chance?"

Elizabeth stared at Kitty, momentarily dumbstruck. Had Kitty read her mind?

Then she collected herself. It had been a random question, not a specific one.

"Handsome friend, Kitty? I cannot think to whom you refer."

"Oh, come on, Lizzy. You don't fool me. Were there any handsome men in the room, or were there not? I do not include Mr. Bingley in that, even though he's handsome, because he's married. Answer the question!"

"She's blushing!" said Mary, with an almost scientific fascination. "See how the colour rises from her cheeks. It almost meets her hairline. Do you see, Kitty?"

"Oh, for goodness' sake." Elizabeth put down her needlework. "Are you thinking of any man in particular, Kitty? Mr. Bingley did indeed introduce us all to a friend of his, who had arrived today with his sister. Mrs. Hurst and Miss Bingley were also there, and had travelled from London with a friend named Miss Carrington. I met no other guests. There. Now you know everything."

"Ooh!" Kitty clapped her hands. "So there *is* a new gentleman in town. I knew it! My maid had some gossip from Netherfield just this morning. Is he as handsome as I hear he is?"

"That is a matter of opinion."

"Is he unmarried?"

"I believe so."

Kitty let out another squeal. "Is he a gentleman of means?"

Elizabeth looked at her pointedly. "Again, I believe he is, but I do not have any details. Let us not gossip about visitors like this, Kitty. Besides, you shall see him at the ball."

"Oh, pish and tish. Gossip is half the fun. I must admit, I'm looking forward to seeing him at the ball, though. Do you think any other suitable bachelors might be there?"

The conversation mercifully turned to the general subject of eligible gentlemen, and Kitty kept up a stream of chatter that left Elizabeth space to compose herself again.

Once more, the mere thought of Mr. Darcy had disturbed her peace. It frustrated her enormously to realise it.

She felt like a calm lake, into which a rock had been thrown. Mr. Darcy was the rock. When made, the ripples took some time to widen and vanish. Until today, she had not even known Mr. Darcy existed. How could he possibly be sliding into every other conversation now?

Picking up her needlework once more, she

threw herself back into the painstaking business of amending the floral edging. She would not think about anything but Longbourn and family, for the rest of the night.

That, she resolved, was that.

CHAPTER 9

"What do you make of Miss Bennet?"

Bingley refreshed his friend's port glass. Just the two gentlemen remained at table, the ladies having retired some time ago.

"Miss Bennet?" Darcy stalled before answering, so he could choose the right words. He did not wish to give in to his friend's good-natured teasing. "Well, your elder sister-in-law seems like a reasonably agreeable young lady."

"Agreeable? Yes, certainly she is." Bingley's eyes sparkled as he questioned his friend. "I noted you spoke with her before she left Netherfield. Did you find her good company?"

Darcy was only too aware of the direction of Bingley's hint.

"I suppose Miss Bennet might make for good company at a social gathering. If one enjoyed that sort of thing."

"And do you?" Bingley took a sip of his port, and Darcy noticed his friend was now smiling broadly at him. "Do you enjoy that sort of thing? Being in the company of ladies such as Miss Bennet, I mean?"

"Why do you grin in that absurd way, Bingley? Have you a pain somewhere?"

Bingley roared with laughter. "Come now, Darcy. You are avoiding the question. I can only conclude you are quite intrigued by Miss Bennet already."

"Nonsense. I do not even know the girl. What poppycock you do talk this evening, Bingley." Darcy knocked back his port and replaced the glass on the table. He stood and moved to the window, looking out at the moonlit gardens beyond.

Bingley's tone turned softer. "Merely a light-hearted remark, Darcy. I do not mean to offend."

"I know." Darcy turned back to his friend, whose smile had been replaced by a look of concern. "Forgive my impatience, Bingley. It has been a trying few months, and I fear I am not yet rehabilitated into polite society."

"Of course. Say no more, old fellow." Bingley poured more port into Darcy's glass, and topped up his own. "I shall not tease you a moment longer about the single ladies of this parish."

"Thank you."

"We shall move on to pastures new, in conversational terms."

"That would be much appreciated." Darcy sat back in his seat and took up his glass.

Mr. Bingley raised his own cheerfully. "How is Miss Darcy now? She seemed well enough when you arrived."

"She is well, but it has been a long road to recovery. For a long while, I feared I would lose her."

"It must have been an awful experience for her. For both of you. Did they ever find the man who tried to force himself upon her?"

"No." Darcy felt his heart seethe with fury. "I am told he fled on a ship. From there, I believe he may have drowned at sea. That is regrettable. I would have preferred him to have faced the full weight of justice on land."

"Quite so. Most hideous business."

"Please do not speak of Georgiana's ordeal to anyone. She carries the burden of the shock, and would not want to have to talk about it to anyone."

"Say no more, my friend. I would not dream of uttering a single word on the topic."

The men sat in amicable silence for a few minutes, until Bingley spoke again.

"I must apologise again for my questions about Miss Bennet, Darcy. It is simply that Mrs. Bingley has been wondering if Miss Bennet might soon find a good match. She is eager to see her beloved sister as happy as she." His face lit up as he spoke of his wife. "I noticed Miss Bennet talking to you earlier, you see, and you seemed most engaged. My sister Mrs. Hurst mentioned some time ago that you had been considering finding a wife. All in all, I put two and two together and made five. Forgive my enthusiasm."

"Mrs. Hurst misremembers our exchange," Darcy said, clasping his hands behind his back. "Upon our last meeting, *she* recommended I find a wife as soon as possible, for she said she believed Pemberley needed a mistress. Miss Bingley agreed with her. *I*, on the other hand, merely noted Mrs. Hurst's opinion, and thanked her for taking the trouble to offer it. I most assuredly did not join her in the sentiment."

"I see."

Darcy took a sip of his port, with a scowl. "As far as Miss Bennet is concerned, I scarcely remember what was said by either of us. Except that I asked her to dance at the ball, but that was a matter of politeness. It was a few moments of idle chatter. Nothing more."

"Understood." Bingley gave his friend a knowing look, and questioned him no further.

Darcy had been the one to change the subject, but for some reason he found his thoughts returning to Miss Bennet. Her lively eyes and quick wit had inflamed him in a most infuriating way. From their limited interaction, he was sure that she would be entertaining company on the dance floor.

However, he had no space in his life for lively eyes, nor intelligent conversation. He simply needed to make up for missing his good friend's wedding. Then he and Georgiana could go back to London. When the season was over, they would return to his Derbyshire estate, and move on with Georgiana's recovery.

The affairs of the mediocre Hertfordshire country set were of limited interest to him, at the best of times. Miss Bennet may have piqued his interest today, but such intrigues never lasted. He was certain it would have waned by the end of the ball. That would suit him perfectly.

"I expect that your young sister will be one of the few ladies not looking for a husband tomorrow, Darcy. Half of the county will be hoping for a match."

"Is it not always so? I have learned to ignore most of the fuss and nonsense."

"Do you have plans for Georgiana's debut?"

"She is not ready yet. I hope in time that she will be sufficiently recovered to make her debut, but perhaps that will have to wait until next year. Perhaps even the year after. There is no hurry, after all."

"Does she wish to be out in society?"

"Yes, as any young girl does. She longs to return to normal life generally. While I have some concerns about launching her back into the world so soon, I know she was looking forward to visiting Netherfield with great fervour. Of course, she would not be parted from me even if she had not been wholly ready." Darcy sipped his port. "She will, by necessity, be confined to her bedchamber during the ball, as she has not been presented in society yet. But it will be a comfort to her to know that I am on the premises."

"Splendid." Bingley raised his port glass and tapped it against Darcy's glass, by way of emphasis. "If Miss Darcy should need anything, please do not hesitate to ask. By all means ask her to speak to Mrs. Bingley directly, if her request should require the attention of a female. We are both anxious to make her welcome, and to shield her from any difficulties she may encounter."

"I appreciate your kindness and generosity, Bingley."

There was a soft knock at the door, then the door opened quietly. It was Mr. Bingley's steward.

"What is it, Mr. Grindle?"

"I am sorry to bother you at this late hour, sir. We are preparing the house for the ball, and we have run into difficulties."

Mr. Bingley sat up straighter. "Difficulties? How so? Has Mrs. Bingley not given you any instructions?"

"She has, sir. Mrs. Bingley has given us most useful, comprehensive instructions. Unfortunately we also have a set of conflicting instructions, and it is proving difficult to marry the two."

"Conflicting instructions? From whom?"

Mr. Grindle looked embarrassed. "From Mrs. Hurst and Miss Bingley, sir. Mrs. Bingley advised that I come to consult you to settle the matter."

Mr. Bingley stood up at once, his face darkening. "Mrs. Bingley is your mistress. You have no other. I do not know what my sisters think they are doing, but they have no right to intervene. Please continue on the path set by the lady of the house. There is no need to consult me again on this. Simply ignore any instructions you are given by anybody else. I will deal with my sisters myself."

"Yes sir." Mr. Grindle bowed and backed out of the room, closing the door after himself.

"Outrageous," Bingley said, pacing the floor. "My sisters are quite out of control."

Darcy nodded. He agreed with his friend's assessment. "It would be advisable to nip this in the bud, Bingley. Your wife has supreme authority over household matters, as you say. Regardless of that, your sisters think that their superior breeding gives them precedence, and it is not so. They must be put in their place."

"Indeed. I simply cannot have my wife undermined in her own home."

Darcy handed Bingley his glass. His friend took it, still frowning.

"We should return to the ladies now, Darcy. I shall take my sisters aside for a dressing-down. Perhaps you would entertain Mrs. Bingley for a while?"

"I should be delighted." Darcy had no great desire to make conversation with anyone but Bingley, but Mrs. Bingley seemed amiable enough, and easy company. Besides, he would have done it even if she had been the most disagreeable creature on earth. He would do anything his friend wanted, if it were within his power. He had missed Bingley's wedding, and for that he could never fully atone.

"Capital. To the drawing room, then."

They took their port glasses and made their way through the adjoining rooms to the place where the ladies sat. Mr. Darcy followed Mr. Bingley's lead, trying to put the thought of a ballroom full of matrimony-obsessed females out of his mind.

Only a few more days before he and Georgiana could escape to London. The time could not fly soon enough for him. At least, that is what he *thought* he felt. His inner sentiments told a different story.

CHAPTER 10

Bingley took his sisters into the library, while Darcy stood before Mrs. Bingley and Miss Carrington.

"Have you been to Hertfordshire before, Miss Carrington?" Darcy began. For her part, Miss Carrington looked utterly terrified to be spoken to directly.

"No. No, I have not." She grew pale, with two pink circles in the middle of each cheek. No more response was forthcoming.

"It is a picturesque part of the country," Jane offered, by way of rescue. She smiled at Miss Carrington. "I hope you will join us in a walk on the morning after the ball. When the sun comes up and the ball ends, we plan a walk around the grounds to usher in the last hours of Christmas-tide."

"That sounds…" Miss Carrington seemed to be grappling for the words. "Um… invigorating."

"Invigorating indeed," Darcy agreed. The conversation was not running smoothly, despite his best efforts and those of the kind-hearted Mrs. Bingley.

He decided to turn his attentions to Mrs. Bingley instead, in the hope that Miss Carrington would join in somewhere when she felt able.

"How do you find Netherfield, Mrs. Bingley?"

"It is a glorious place." Her eyes shone as she surveyed the room they were in. "Such a hand-somely-proportioned building, and many acres of fine land. Mr. Bingley has a great many plans for the fields yonder."

"Does he intend to buy a house in future? Perhaps he would even make an offer to buy Netherfield?"

"I believe he is happy enough to rent the house for the foreseeable future." Mrs. Bingley smiled to herself. "Of course, if anything were to change, perhaps he would consider his options once more."

Her enigmatic smile was not lost on Darcy. His eyes flicked down to Mrs. Bingley's hands, twisting in her lap, then back to her face. She looked both serene and excited, if that were even possible. What did she mean by "if anything were to change"?

He suddenly had an inkling what she might mean. Was she hinting that she was expecting Mr. Bingley's heir?

Her dress was cut in the modern style, with a high waist and fabric flowing more loosely over the hips, so he could not tell if there were any swelling in the area. Yet there was something in the rosy bloom of her cheeks which made him think he had accidentally hit upon the right answer.

To his astonishment, Darcy found himself feeling proud of his younger friend, and hoping for Bingley's sake that his wife was indeed with child.

He found his own response unexpected, because he was usually indifferent to other people's reproductive impulses. Indeed, he had none at all of his own. News of his friends' children usually passed him by. He could not tell why he was suddenly receptive to the idea of his friend becoming a father.

"I trust that Mr. Bingley will make all the right decisions regarding any future outcomes," he said. It was a vague and meaningless statement, but it seemed to make Mrs. Bingley happy. Her eyes shone as she agreed with him.

"And will you consider settling down soon, Mr. Darcy?"

There it was again. The question he always spent a great deal of time trying to evade.

It was quite proper for a married woman such as Mrs. Bingley to ask it, and he was under no illusion that he should be spared his hosts' curiosity, especially as they were still basking in newlywed joy. A single man of means would never be able to mix with others without that question being—at the very least—thought. Among close friends, it would almost certainly be asked.

"I have made no plans of any kind, Mrs. Bingley, other than to return to London on the seventh day of January, and to spend the rest of the season there."

"Oh, of course. Well, perhaps you will find a bride in London! Or perhaps you might find one in a more unexpected place. We never know what life may offer us, do we, Mr. Darcy?"

"Quite so." Mr. Darcy sidestepped the subject, as he always did, and diverted the conversation's course elsewhere. "I understand from your sister Miss Bennet that your father has lately been unwell? Please accept my best wishes for a complete and speedy recovery."

"Thank you." Mrs. Bingley's face fell as she contemplated her father's health. A tiny needle of guilt pricked at Darcy's conscience. That was a poor choice of topic. He had succeeded in distracting her from his matrimonial prospects, but at the expense of her cheerful mood.

His regret did not linger for long. At that moment, the door burst open and Mrs. Hurst and Miss Bingley charged in, followed by a rather angry looking Bingley.

"We are most terribly sorry for intruding on your duties, Mrs. Bingley, and we promise not to attempt to usurp your authority again at any time." Miss Bingley offered her apology in a sharp, angry tone. Bingley glowered over her as she delivered it.

"Yes, indeed," added Mrs. Hurst, who looked sulky.

Neither woman seemed sincerely contrite, but they had evidently accepted that they were in the wrong.

"Let us forget this matter altogether," Mrs. Bingley suggested, with her usual mild tone. "No harm has been done."

Her emollient tone seemed to calm things substantially. The ladies began to exchange small talk, and it seemed that all was well.

Bingley caught Darcy's eye and nodded pointedly at him, as if to say "It is done". Darcy nodded back approvingly.

"Perhaps Miss Bingley would now play us something on the pianoforte?" Mrs. Bingley suggested, undoubtedly eager to restore an amiable atmosphere.

Miss Bingley agreed to this, and threw herself down onto the piano stool next to her sister-in-law. Mrs. Hurst sat beside Mrs. Bingley, with a smile that did not seem entirely natural.

Darcy and Bingley drifted together and began a conversation audible only to themselves. The ladies were left to entertain each other as they did so.

CHAPTER 11

The next morning was the coldest of the winter so far. Frost glittered across the lawn and hedgerows, and ice had formed on the insides of the windows. The sky was a crumpled sheet of dove-grey. A cobweb on the outside of Elizabeth's chamber window-frame sparkled, as though jewelled with a thousand tiny diamonds.

The servants had been up early stoking the fires, but they shivered as they moved through the unheated hallway to access the fire-lit rooms. Each Bennet sister dressed in many layers, and wrapped herself in a thick shawl.

Elizabeth slept longer than usual, and rose late. As Mary had predicted, Mrs. Bennet was downstairs by the time Elizabeth reached the dining room. Breakfast had already begun.

Usually, Elizabeth had a couple of hours to spend as she wished before breakfast was served, so this was a late start for her indeed.

Mrs. Bennet greeted her daughter as though she, Mrs. Bennet, had not been in bed for days. She did not mention her absence in passing, and neither did she attempt to excuse or explain it in any way.

"Good morning, dear. These chops are uncommonly tender. Are they not, Mary?" She nodded at her own question, before Mary could answer. "Come and sit beside me, Lizzy."

Elizabeth obeyed. She had not expected anything else from her temperamental mother, so Elizabeth too behaved as though nothing had happened.

"Good morning, Mamma. I am glad to see you well today."

"Oh yes. Quite well, dear, quite well. Now then, look out of the window. It will snow today, Lizzy, just you wait and see."

She took a bite of her chop, and continued to speak with her mouth full. Elizabeth winced.

"Does Jane need any help with arrangements for the ball? I hear there are to be many guests staying at Netherfield for Twelfth Night. Many gentlemen, if I'm not much mistaken. Keep your eyes sharp and your focus wide, girls. Jane may yet play match-maker." Her eyes widened and she nodded again, this time suggestively, at Elizabeth. "Perhaps it is not yet too late for you to find a husband, Lizzy."

Elizabeth sighed to herself. Not again. She had had enough of that sentiment from Kitty the previous night. "Why *should* it be too late, Mamma? I am but one-and-twenty, after all! There is no reason why it should take years for me to find a suitable husband. And even if it did, surely there is no age limit on love?"

"Love, indeed. *Love*." Mrs. Bennet snorted. "Love will not put meat and drink on the table, dear girl. Believe me when I tell you that marrying a reliable gentleman with a good income brings a far happier home than any measure of *love* can secure." She glared at her plate. "Anyway, perhaps there shall be someone suitable for you at Netherfield this Twelfth Night."

Elizabeth knew her mother was speaking of her own situation when she dismissed marrying for love. As a lawyer's daughter, her mother had risen in the social ranks when she married a gentleman of superior social standing. Yet Mr. Bennet had been reckless with money, and their home would be lost to Mr. Collins upon Mr. Bennet's passing. Sadly, Mr. Bennet had failed to provide continuous security for his family. So Mrs. Bennet evidently considered the match had not been ideal.

Elizabeth could understand her mother's frustration. She loved her father dearly, but if his four unmarried daughters did not find suitable matches, he would leave them in a precarious position. It was most fortunate that Jane had married a man of means, for Elizabeth knew Mr. Bingley would not see them destitute. Elizabeth would not wish to impose on his kindness, however. The costs of maintaining four unmarried ladies and a widow would be considerable.

In any case, she hoped that Mr. Bennet would live a long and happy life, and none of this would be a consideration. Similarly, if they were all married before he left the earthly realm, the problem would never arise. Any one of them then could take care of their mother. Jane and Mr. Bingley would not be left with the responsibility of maintaining six additional people.

"And as for Lydia—*well.*" Mrs. Bennet helped

herself to a kidney, stabbing at it furiously with a fork. "That girl will be the death of me. Off she goes, without a care in the world, with that dreadful draper's daughter. What Lydia sees in that silly friend of hers, I have no idea. And where is she staying? With whom is she consorting? *That* I would like to know."

"We all would," Elizabeth agreed, slicing her chop thoughtfully. "Do we not have a record of the friend's address?"

"I could look through her bedchamber and check if she left her diary at home?" offered Kitty.

"Nosy thing," snapped Mrs. Bennet. "Well, if we have no other options, yes, we shall have to look in the girl's diary. Not knowing where she has gone is intolerable. I *must* know where my poor foolish Lydia is."

Lydia had always been Mrs. Bennet's favourite, and Elizabeth could see how much the girl's disappearance had affected her mother. Mrs. Bennet seemed back to normal in most respects, but her eyes remained red and swollen, as though she had cried a lot during the last few days.

Elizabeth felt a wave of sympathy for her

mother. She was truly only trying to do her best for them all, even if her methods were often not to Elizabeth's liking. Her brashness was inadvertent, and her intentions were good. She resolved to be more patient with Mamma from then on.

"Mother, will you attend Jane's ball?" Mary asked.

"Of course! Good heavens. You surely don't imagine I would miss it, do you? Why, it shall be quite the finest social gathering Hertfordshire has known these last twelve months! We are honoured, *honoured,* that such a fine gentleman as Mr. Bingley has consented to hold his Twelfth Night ball in our little part of the countryside. He could have made just as gay a time of it in London. We must not forget that."

"Yes, I am glad too," Kitty said. "I shall wear my new whitework gown. Perhaps I might meet a dashing gentleman of my own! What do you think, Mamma? Would you like to see me married before the new year is out?"

"I should view it as exceedingly fortunate, if any man would have you." Mrs. Bennet chopped up her eggs with vigour. "But we must get Lizzy and Mary married off first."

"Oh, don't make me wait for those two to find

husbands!" Kitty looked outraged. "Lizzy is far too fussy, and Mary will never be married. She was born an eternal spinster. *Look* at her."

Mary frowned at Kitty over her breakfast, clearly hurt.

"Don't be unkind, Kitty," Elizabeth said. "Mary has as much chance of a happy match as any of us do. And we shall all enjoy the ball, whether or not we find our future husbands there."

"If only Lydia were here," Kitty said, gazing out of the window. "We always have a splendid time together at social events. It will not be the same without her. Do you think she might return in time for Twelfth Night?"

"I hope so." Elizabeth thought that would be very agreeable indeed, though she had little hope of its occurring. "But we should accept that she may be celebrating Epiphany with her friend's family, as she is not back yet. Sooner or later, she will remember her duty to us and send us a letter. I am sure of it."

"She had better do that," Mrs. Bennet said, looking furious. "The worry I have had over that girl! It is bad enough that she has absconded with the daughter of a tradesman. If she has been mixing with even lower company, I shall be aggrieved. *Very* aggrieved."

Elizabeth took her mother's hand. "Do not worry, Mamma. Lydia will be all right. She will come home soon."

She wished she felt as confident as she sounded. Nevertheless, she had to reassure her mother, regardless of her own private doubts. Any concerns she had must be kept strictly to herself.

"Are Mr. Bingley's sisters staying at Netherfield?" asked her mother dabbing her mouth with a napkin.

"They are. Both arrived yesterday, with a friend of the family."

"Ooh!" Mrs. Bennet sat up straight. "What of this *friend*?"

"A young lady named Miss Carrington. She seems quiet, but amiable enough."

Mrs. Bennet slumped back in her chair. "Pah. A young lady. I had hoped you were going to say it was a gentleman. Perhaps a cousin of Mr. Bingley, or someone we had not yet met."

Elizabeth smiled. "Patience, Mamma. There will be plenty of gentlemen at the ball, and you may size them all up then."

She chewed a mouthful of food and paused. Should she tell her mother about Mr. Darcy? He was an eligible bachelor, after all. She would certainly be interested to learn of him.

Upon a few moments' consideration, she decided against it. It would excite Mrs. Bennet's hopes, and all for nothing. Mr. Darcy was not the sort of gentleman who would be looking to marry a daughter from a simple country family like theirs. He would have women a-plenty to choose from, over the length and breadth of the country.

Kitty, regrettably, had other ideas.

"Aren't you going to tell Mamma about Mr. Darcy?" Kitty gave her elder sister a sly smile. "Perhaps she hopes to keep him all to herself."

"Nonsense, Kitty." Elizabeth noticed her heart pounding faster as the matter was raised, and it irritated her. "Mamma, Mr. Bingley also brought a friend, named Mr. Darcy. He has a younger sister. There. Now it is all said."

"Mr. Darcy?" It was as though Mrs. Bennet's ears had pricked up, like those of a hound. "Tell me more. Is he a single man?"

"Yes. He is single, handsome and rich. May we move on, please?"

"Look! Lizzy's blushing again. She cannot speak of this gentleman without turning claret-red. What does that tell you, Mamma?" Kitty clapped her hands with glee. "She admits he is handsome too. I think we have a match!"

Elizabeth threw down her napkin and stood up. "This is ridiculous. I am tired of hearing of eligible gentlemen, and I beg leave to be excused. I shall take up some food to Father."

She filled a plate haphazardly and placed a knife and fork on the side.

It would be a bad idea to sit around at Longbourn today. Kitty was enjoying making her squirm about Mr. Darcy, and Elizabeth hated the idea that she was unable to stop her face from reddening when his name was mentioned. She was not a silly young girl, and was quite ashamed of herself for conducting herself like one. Perhaps a trip out of doors would cure her.

Was there any errand she could undertake, by way of a reasonable excuse to leave the house?

Of course! She needed some new white evening gloves for the ball. One of hers was fraying at the inner seam, and had been repaired too many times to be re-stitched again successfully. That was settled. She would walk into Meryton to purchase a new pair.

The pale winter sun had come out, and the frost would begin to clear within the hour. It would be a bracing walk, but she could wrap up warmly, and the fresh air would do her no end of good.

Before Mrs. Bennet could quiz her further on the marriageability of Mr. Darcy, she curtseyed and headed to the door. She would be glad to visit her father. He would understand her need for escape.

Her mother called after her. "Tell me one thing, Lizzy dear. Do you like this Mr. Darcy at all?"

"I must take this to Father," Elizabeth called, as she hurried out of the room.

Balancing the plate in one hand, she closed the door behind her, and fled.

CHAPTER 12

Darcy's attempts to travel alone with his sister to Meryton were thwarted at every turn. According to his host's sisters, it was quite unthinkable that the Darcys should make their visit to the village unaccompanied. Miss Bingley was especially eager to protect them from this fate.

"Meryton? Oh, what a good idea, Mr. Darcy. Mrs. Hurst, Miss Carrington and I shall be delighted to join you. My friend always seizes the chance to take some fresh air. She is so very mindful of her health, you see."

Darcy reined in his exasperation. "I understood that you all intended to tour Netherfield with your brother this morning, Miss Bingley?"

Miss Bingley smiled sweetly. "Oh, we can

amble around the estate tomorrow after the ball instead. I see no need to do so now. Our brother also has a lot of dull estate business to attend to, which we would be ecstatic to avoid. Besides, Miss Carrington would much rather visit Meryton than traipse around a boring old garden. Is that not so, dear?"

Miss Carrington stared, with wide eyes, and stuttered "Oh, I…"

Her friend glared at her.

Miss Carrington managed to add a half-whispered "Yes, thank you," before clamming up once more.

Darcy bowed. He could make no further objection without appearing rude, and was therefore forced to accept Bingley's sisters and their friend as members of their party. They would all travel in the carriage to Meryton together. It would be considered proper because of the presence of Mrs. Hurst, a married woman. She could act as chaperone.

Just so long as Georgiana buys the things she needs, he told himself. He was sure he could endure a few hours of Bingley's sisters' chatter, for Georgiana's sake. It would not be easy, though.

"Oh, we shall have such fun showing you the village!" Miss Bingley went on, oblivious to Darcy's disdainful expression. "It is full of boorish locals, naturally, but even so, it possesses a certain charm. Might I enquire as to the nature of your visit? Did you wish to buy something in particular, sir?"

"My sister wishes to make some purchases. My only wish is that we undertake the task with the minimum possible fuss."

Miss Bingley nodded, and patted her bonnet. "Very well. I shall get ready at once. Miss Carrington, please join me upstairs. We must not detain Mr. Darcy any further. Mr. Darcy, we shall be delighted to meet you here once more in ten minutes. We shall delay you no longer than that."

Darcy bowed graciously, already wishing the excursion finished.

To remain within the bounds of etiquette, he had no choice but to take the three ladies with them. He could not snub the sisters of his oldest friend, and it may be useful for Georgiana to have the attentions of a female, if she needed to buy anything of a particularly feminine nature. He was more than happy to fund her shopping trip, but he would be of little use if she needed a second opinion on a pair of court shoes.

Twenty minutes later, Miss Bingley, Mrs. Hurst and Miss Carrington returned, and Darcy was circumspect enough not to mention the excess time taken.

Mr. Bingley had purchased a new closed carriage shortly after his marriage. "The chaise-and-four was a young man's vehicle," he had told Mr. Darcy. That morning, his house-guests Mr. Darcy, Miss Darcy, Mrs. Hurst, Miss Bingley and Miss Carrington all climbed inside, remarking on its comfort and Mr. Bingley's good taste.

The carriage seated four extremely comfort-ably, and five at a slight squeeze, with ample room on top for any parcels they may choose to bring back, rather than leave to the delivery boy. Mr. Darcy and his sister sat on one side, and Mrs. Hurst, Miss Bingley and Miss Carrington took their places on the opposite seat.

Georgiana squeezed her brother's hand. "What a lovely carriage!" she said, happily.

Darcy felt a warm surge of relief in his heart when he saw her big, genuine smile. He was glad her spirits were cheered by the morning's activi-ties, at least for now.

"Oh, there's something else. Mr. Hurst is due to arrive at Netherfield this afternoon, after all," Mrs. Hurst announced, as the carriage glided down the long driveway. "His plans have changed, and he is now able to attend the ball. We are all so pleased."

"Naturally."

"Of course, it does mean we will have less time to talk together," Miss Bingley added. "But at least I have my dear Jemima here too. She shall make sure I am entertained!"

Miss Carrington looked startled at this, but gave a meek smile and said nothing.

By the time they reached Meryton and exited the carriage, Georgiana was laughing with Miss Carrington, and seemed very relaxed. Perhaps it was all for the best that the two other ladies were there. Darcy would stand back and allow them to take Georgiana under their collective wing. It would make a nice change for her.

Out of the corner of his eye, Darcy spotted a figure moving in the distance. The person was silhouetted against the low winter sun, so he couldn't make it out fully, but it bore the shape of a female, and looked somehow familiar. Miss

Bingley spotted his curious frown, and followed his gaze.

"Oh, good lord. That's not... Is that Miss Bennet?" Miss Bingley shaded her eyes from the sun with one hand. "It is, is it not?"

Darcy's heart jumped in his chest as he realised she was right. It was Miss Bennet. There she was, as large as life. It was almost as though he had conjured her from his mind, because she had kept appearing in there since the moment they had met. He was still entirely oblivious as to the meaning of this.

On the other side of the street marched the young lady, with purposeful intent. Her cheeks were pink, and her hems and boots were edged in mud. One stray curl bobbed around her neck, having escaped her bonnet.

Darcy had a sudden urge to coil the disobedient lock around his fingers and tuck it back into its place. He quelled it.

"Yes, it is Miss Bennet," Georgiana agreed. "Shall we ask her to join us?"

"Oh, I don't think so," said Miss Bingley, at once.

"No need," Mrs. Hurst said, instantly.

"Of course we shall," said Darcy, simultaneously.

Georgiana took her brother's response as the correct one. She scampered over to Miss Bennet, and Darcy noted the exact moment when the muddy young lady recognised Georgiana. Miss Bennet's warm smile to his sister made him smile involuntarily too, for a second.

"Look at the state of her petticoats. Did she *walk* into the village?" Miss Bingley squawked, in an incredulous tone. "How perfectly undignified."

Darcy ignored her, for he was pleasantly occupied in watching Miss Bennet trudge her way over to them, muddy petticoats and all. He bowed, and drank in the sight of her curtseying in her mud-streaked outfit.

It looked as though the morning was going to turn out to be much less dull than he had feared.

"MY GOODNESS, Miss Bennet. Look at your boots! One might almost think you marched your way here down muddy lanes, instead of taking a carriage." Miss Bennet held Miss Bingley's eye with confidence, and just a little defiance. "Surely not?"

"I did indeed walk here, Miss Bingley. It is a perfectly lovely day for a walk."

She was certainly spirited, Darcy thought, smiling against his will. He reflected on the way Miss Bennet held her own against Miss Bingley, compared with the meek compliance of Miss Carrington. That little mouse shrank back behind her bolder friend, and said nothing, even when Miss Bingley was sharp with her.

"Oh, how funny. I don't think I have ever seen a lady in such disarray." Miss Bingley gave a shrill laugh.

Miss Carrington remained silent and frozen to the spot, so Miss Bingley nudged her sharply in the ribs. It appeared that she had been expected to back up Miss Bingley's reaction. But she did not. Even with the violent prompt, she remained silent. Darcy gave her credit for withstanding the pressure, at least.

Miss Bennet gave a curt smile. "Ah, it is very obvious how much you must enjoy your time in London, Miss Bingley. Here in the country, we take great pleasure in the sights and sounds of nature. A bracing walk is a fine way to obtain both. We are not so fragile that a little wet earth scares us."

"Would you want your sister to walk miles down country lanes, Mr. Darcy?" Miss Bingley asked, turning to him with an innocent half-smile. "Would you think that was becoming conduct?"

"If she wished to do so, I would not stand in her way."

Miss Bennet's mouth turned up almost imperceptibly at the corners.

Miss Bingley's brow furrowed. "And you'd let your wife to do the same? If you were married, I mean. You'd allow your wife to step in puddles up to her ankles and walk around like a drowned rat, would you?"

"As you acknowledge, I do not have a wife, so this line of questioning is futile."

"I know that, Mr. Darcy. But when you do?"

"I will not, and I shall not."

All four women stared at him. He began to feel most irritated. Miss Bingley grabbed his arm too, which only served to annoy him further.

"You cannot give up so easily, Mr. Darcy! The right woman might be just around the—"

Darcy interrupted her, detaching his arm

from her grasp. "It is not a matter of giving up. I do not *wish* to find a wife, Miss Bingley. Not now. Not ever."

Miss Carrington looked shocked, and Georgiana slipped her arm into hers. Miss Bingley glared at Darcy, while Miss Bennet looked on curiously.

"Come now, Mr. Darcy. You don't mean that," Miss Bingley said.

"I am afraid I do, Miss Bingley. Wives are a joy to many gentlemen, I'm sure, but so are spaniels. I have no need of either."

The ladies were all rendered speechless. It was as if Mr. Darcy had expressed a dislike of music, or candlelight. The whole sentiment was quite unthinkable.

For a moment, the conversation foundered. Then Miss Bennet spoke.

"This has been a most pleasant interlude, but I regret I must go now. Please excuse me, sir. Forgive me, ladies. I must make a purchase this very day, and I beg your leave to do so now."

"Well, of course. But what is it you need to buy, Miss Bennet?" Miss Bingley tipped her head to one side, as though deeply fascinated by the subject. Darcy wondered if he was imagining the mischief in her tone. He doubted it.

"Gloves, Miss Bingley. I need to buy new evening gloves."

"Oh, marvellous. Pray, let me accompany you. My sister, Miss Darcy and Miss Carrington will be quite all right together while we go, won't you dears?"

The three other ladies nodded, and glanced at one another. It almost appeared to Darcy that Georgiana and Miss Carrington looked relieved. He could hardly blame his sister for that.

Before Miss Bennet could respond, Miss Bingley linked arms with her and marched her off in the direction of the shop. Miss Bennet looked back over her shoulder, as if she had something more to say to Darcy, but Miss Bingley was too swift, and Miss Bennet turned back again.

Mr. Darcy smiled at his sister. "Come now, Georgiana. Let us browse and buy what you need."

Unbeknownst to the others, Darcy could not avoid feeling that he wished Miss Bennet was on his side of the party, and not the other. He refused to examine the feeling, and instead pushed it aside.

He did not speak the sentiment aloud, but Darcy guessed they probably all found the excursion a little more agreeable from that moment on. The three of them strolled toward the draper's shop in companionable silence.

CHAPTER 13

Elizabeth had made it as clear as she could that she did not seek the company of Miss Bingley. But decorum meant she could not go any further. Consequently, she was at the end of her abilities to influence the situation, and was not sure how to rid herself of her unwanted companion. The only possible outcome was that she would just have to endure her presence.

"I am sure that you have more important things to do here in Meryton," Elizabeth said to Miss Bingley, but to no avail.

She did not want to go shopping with Miss Bingley. Not in the slightest. But she could not refuse without being rude.

Reluctantly, she accepted Miss Bingley's presence with a cool smile. The two of them walked together to view some gloves in the shop window.

"I expect Mr. Darcy will be grateful for our leaving him to Miss Carrington's company," Miss Bingley said, with a knowing smirk.

Elizabeth glanced along the line of gloves on display behind glass. "How so?"

"Well, isn't it obvious? Mr. Darcy is in love with Miss Carrington. He is just biding his time before proposing."

Elizabeth had not received that impression at all, and she could not understand why Miss Bingley had. She examined an elbow-length white glove in the shop window, trying to calm her heart. It was racing oddly.

"How curious. Mr. Darcy just told us all that he wished never to marry."

Miss Bingley laughed uproariously. "Oh, my dear! You did not believe that, did you? Mr. Darcy is merely trying to cover his own tracks in this regard."

Elizabeth frowned at her companion. "In what regard?"

"Mr. Darcy does not want Miss Carrington to become complacent, though his intentions are obvious! It is the way these gentleman conduct themselves. They like to throw the ladies off the scent, so they can take them by surprise later in the manner of their proposal."

"That sounds awfully convoluted. Why does Mr. Darcy not speak to Miss Carrington directly and make his intentions clear, if he has any?"

"What would be the fun in that?" Miss Bingley chuckled again, leaving Elizabeth even more perplexed.

Was this really how rich gentlemen like Mr. Darcy conducted themselves? Did ladies of Miss Bingley's class all know about this? Elizabeth felt as though she had visited another world for the day, instead of just the village she had been visiting all her life.

Miss Bingley sighed deeply. "I daresay you are as surprised as I am about Mr. Darcy's liking for Miss Carrington. She is quite outside his usual type, too. He usually prefers tall, fine-boned ladies, so I am given to understand."

Elizabeth noted wryly to herself that Miss Bingley was, by pure coincidence, tall and fine-boned.

"I confess, Miss Bingley, the tale is a tad confusing. I do not know quite how anyone could gain a good overview of Mr. Darcy's preferences, when he claims to have rejected love altogether."

"Heavens, Miss Bennet, you are such a country girl! You have clearly spent hardly any time in London since your debut. Those of us well versed in society know that the path of love never runs in a straight line. And it is all the more enjoyable for it."

Elizabeth had actually spent some time in London, but not a great deal, so she could not contradict Miss Bingley fully. She remained silent, and simply examined the items for sale again. The long white gloves in the window drew her eye once more, and she made to enter the shop.

To Elizabeth's dismay, Miss Bingley followed her inside too.

"Did you have a pleasant conversation with Mr. Darcy at Netherfield yesterday?" she said.

Apparently Miss Bingley had no intention of letting the subject drop.

Elizabeth concentrated on keeping her tone light and friendly, and her eyes on the merchandise.

"Yes, although not very much conversation was had. We merely exchanged pleasantries."

There was a brief pause, before Miss Bingley resumed the conversation.

"I am rather *hoping* Mr. Darcy marries Miss Carrington, as I am sure you must have guessed."

Elizabeth stared at her. None of what Miss Bingley was saying made any sense.

Mr. Darcy had given no impression of having been in any way interested in Miss Carrington, and the lack of interest seemed to be mutual. In fact, Elizabeth had always supposed that *Miss Bingley* had designs on Mr. Darcy. Miss Bingley certainly took every opportunity to direct her most winning smiles at him, and she gave every impression of being rather determined to win his good favour. So why on earth was she talking in this way?

"Indeed?" was all Elizabeth could think to mutter in response.

"Oh yes. Miss Carrington and Mr. Darcy would be a great match, wouldn't you say? Unless there is someone else you think would be a better option?"

Miss Bingley's smile was sly, and her words seemed to be leading somewhere unknown. Elizabeth knew it would be wise to back away from this strange discussion altogether.

"I'm afraid I have been too distracted with my parents' indisposition to think of Mr. Darcy's marriage prospects," she said. "Now, if you'll excuse me, I simply must attend to my purchases."

Miss Bingley could say no more, because a shopgirl approached Elizabeth, with a welcoming curtsey. Her conversation was unavoidably stalled.

Elizabeth was immensely relieved, and threw herself wholeheartedly into the business of browsing gloves. She hoped Miss Bingley would have grown tired of gossip by the time they had finished. If she finished this transaction promptly, she could be back on the open road and enjoying another crisp winter walk within ten minutes. The thought was very appealing.

ELIZABETH ASKED to try on the gloves, and the assistant found the correct size for her. They were lovely indeed. The tops of the gloves skirted her upper arm, ruching delicately at the elbow when she bent it. All in all, they would be perfect for formal occasions.

"I shall take them," Elizabeth told the young lady, who beamed delightedly and took the gloves to wrap.

Elizabeth's companion continued to stand next to her throughout the transaction. It was most disconcerting.

"Of course, Miss Carrington is equally enraptured with Mr. Darcy," she began again.

Elizabeth rolled her eyes. Here they were again.

Miss Bingley seemed to be determined to convince her that Mr. Darcy and Miss Carrington would soon be betrothed. There was obviously a reason for that. Did she suspect Elizabeth was affected by his presence?

No, it was not that. She would have been much more pointed about her remarks if she had. No, it had to be to do with the fact that Miss Bingley herself was interested in Mr. Darcy. Elizabeth had got that impression the moment he walked in. Could this odd story about Miss Carrington be designed in some way to cover her tracks? It was inexplicable beyond that, but Miss Bingley was a complicated sort of person.

"How lovely," Elizabeth said, keeping her

voice light. " I am sure they will be most happy together."

She was sure that Miss Bingley enjoyed the competitive nature of somebody disagreeing with her, so Elizabeth was determined to agree with everything she said, in the hope that it would soon be so dull she would return to her other activities. If she could not convince Miss Bingley to leave by polite means, she would have to just bore her into wandering away.

They left the shop together, Elizabeth tucking the tied paper package under her arm. It had been a rather tiresome fifteen minutes, but at least she now had gloves to wear to the ball.

"Well, I shall not keep you a moment longer," Miss Bingley said, with another mysterious smile. "I am sure you have a long walk ahead of you, and I should not wish to detain you any further."

Elizabeth curtseyed and prepared to take her leave of the party. If the others were elsewhere, she would simply pass on her best wishes through Miss Bingley, and go. Besides, it would suit her if she did not have to come back into contact with Mr. Darcy. It seemed to agitate her somewhat. She was sorry not to say goodbye to

Miss Darcy, and to Miss Carrington, but she knew they would understand.

Unfortunately, at that very moment, Mr. Darcy, Miss Darcy, Mrs. Hurst and Miss Carrington all returned to the centre of the village where Miss Bingley and Elizabeth stood. Miss Darcy waved at Elizabeth as they approached, beaming sweetly at her.

"I am sure they will not mind if you go now," Miss Bingley said, swiftly. "They will quite understand. Your journey back to Long-bourn will take quite some time, and it is understandable that you wish to begin it at once."

Elizabeth could tell that Miss Bingley was trying to hurry her away. Though she too wanted to make herself scarce, Miss Bingley's heavy-handed manipulation made her more deter-mined to stay put.

"Have you finished your shopping, Miss Bennet?" Miss Darcy asked.

"Yes, thank you. Miss Bingley was a most attentive companion throughout."

"We were considering taking a walk to the shoe shop together. Would you care to join us?"

Mr. Darcy caught Elizabeth's eye. She felt a

jolt as their eyes looked together, and looked away.

"Thank you, but I shall not impose upon your kindness any longer. I do need to return home and check that my father has everything he needs."

"Are you returning to Longbourn now?" Mr. Darcy asked Elizabeth.

She forced herself to look back at him, and smiled politely. "Yes sir. I have completed all my business in the village, and it is time I made my way home before the light grows more dim."

"Please allow us to drive you home in the carriage," Mr. Darcy said, with a nod. "The sky is heavy, and it would appear that rain is due at any time this afternoon. I should not wish you to be caught in a storm."

"You are too kind." Elizabeth looked up at the dull sky. "But I think the rain will hold off a while longer. The exercise will do me good, and I do enjoy the peace of a country walk, where one might contemplate and reflect without disturbance."

"Nonetheless, I insist."

Their eyes locked once more. Elizabeth saw that he was as stubborn as she.

"Let us not pressure the poor girl into a carriage ride, if she prefers the bracing air of a walk!" Miss Bingley said, with a laugh. "If I were a country girl, *I* should not wish to be forced into a carriage ride if I had my heart set on a stroll through the meadows. And Miss Bennet is certainly a country girl, through and through."

For the first time, Elizabeth found herself grateful for Miss Bingley's interference. She certainly did not wish to endure a ride in the carriage with the man who was responsible for the strange feelings she kept noticing.

Furthermore, the carriage may have fit five people on the way to Meryton, but six was pushing the bounds of comfort. Elizabeth's inclusion would inevitably compel one of the party to sit with the driver, and that would inevitably be Mr. Darcy. She could not in all conscience insist upon his sitting outside when he was wearing quite the finest suit she had ever seen. The fabric alone must have cost a small fortune.

"Then that's settled," Elizabeth said, seizing the opportunity to agree with the domineering Miss Bingley. "I shall walk. Now I must take my leave of you Mr. Darcy, Miss Darcy, and Miss

Bingley. It has been a great pleasure to run into you unexpectedly in this way, and I do hope you enjoy the rest of your day."

When the appropriate curtsies had taken place, and Mr. Darcy had bowed with an unfathomably surly, expression, Elizabeth turned on her heel and set off towards the main road.

It took a good 10 minutes of purposeful walking before her heart calmed down. Mr. Darcy's effect on her was most disagreeable. She did not look forward to having to dance with him first at the ball, but she hoped after that half-hour awkwardness, she would enjoy the rest of the evening.

With every step she took, her sense of calm returned. She would enjoy the journey home from Meryton very much. Before long, she had taken all her cares out of her mind, set them aside, and then replaced them with birdsong. It was a lovely walk indeed.

CHAPTER 14

Elizabeth relished the first twenty minutes of her walk back to Longbourn. It was cold, but the crisp air and the stark wintry scenery invigorated her spirits, and made her glad to be alive. The icy wind shook her bonnet and her petticoats, but she marched on cheerfully regardless.

But those twenty minutes or so really were all she could enjoy. At her next step, a droplet of water hit her in the eye. Another landed on her nose. Elizabeth looked up at the sky, and received an abrupt faceful of cold water. She knew she would soon be drenched by the sudden downpour which had suddenly emerged from the clouds.

Rain was falling hard, hitting the earth with

thuds and splashes. The heavens had well and truly opened. Elizabeth was wrapped up warm to protect against the cold, but she had no protection at all from the rain. The trees nearby were spindly and bare, and provided no shelter.

She picked up the pace, walking as fast as she could, her breath quickening accordingly. The package under her arm, containing her brand-new gloves, was saturated, and the paper was beginning to disintegrate. She tucked it tightly under her cloak, put her head down, and sped up even more. Holding her bonnet firmly against her head, she marched against the suddenly furious wind which now buffeted her this way and that.

She could not have been walking more than five minutes in the rain when she heard horses' hooves from some way behind her. At once, she stepped aside, to allow the vehicle to pass.

"Miss Bennett!"

The voice was familiar. Its deep rumble almost made her jump, because she had not been expecting to hear it. She had left Mr. Darcy in the village, and was quite unsettled to hear his tones once again, here on the lane leading to Longbourn.

Turning towards the carriage, she shaded her eyes against the rain and squinted. The carriage pulled up beside her, and Mr. Darcy leapt out.

"Miss Bennett," he called out, holding open the carriage door. "Please, step inside."

Elizabeth bit her lip, hesitant. She did not wish to accept the offer of a ride in the carriage. She had already made a big show of turning it down.

On the other hand, she was also reluctant to walk in this heavy rain.

"Mr. Darcy, I thank you, but I really could not inconvenience you. Besides, I am sure the rain will stop soon."

"Nonsense." Mr. Darcy looked up at the darkening sky, and shook his head. "There is absolutely no way the rain is going to stop soon. By the looks of things, this torrent will continue all afternoon. You would be wise to find shelter as soon as possible. Do not leave it so long that you come down with a chill."

His authoritative tone irritated Elizabeth beyond measure. She was not at all fond of being told what to do by people she hardly knew, especially when they spoke to her as though she were a silly child.

"I will return home to Longbourn and dry off there. In any case, I am covered in mud and rain now, and would not dream of sullying Mr. Bingley's fine carriage."

"Bingley will not mind," Mr. Darcy said, brushing raindrops from his own face. "He would far rather his sister-in-law got home without catching her death of cold." He turned to address the party inside the carriage. "Would you not say so, Mrs. Hurst?"

Mrs. Hurst simply smiled in response. Miss Bingley looked out of the carriage window at them. "Well, Charles *is* a stickler for cleanliness," she began. Then she smiled, with no feeling transmitted from behind the eyes. "But of course, I am sure Charles would be delighted for you to take a more convenient method of transportation than the one you originally chose, Miss Bennet. After all, any mess you make can be cleaned up by the staff."

Miss Bingley's sour face made it clear what she really thought of this plan, and the message was not lost on Elizabeth.

Miss Darcy and Miss Carrington said nothing, but the looks on their faces made it clear they sympathised with Elizabeth.

"Miss Bennett, this is quite extraordinary." Mr. Darcy sounded perplexed, and rather cross. "As a gentleman, I am duty-bound to ensure a lady's safety and welfare. You cannot walk home in this deluge, Miss Bennet, and that is final."

Elizabeth stood up to her full height. "With the greatest respect, sir, it is not up to you."

Mr. Darcy stood stock-still in front of her, apparently taken aback at her response. The two of them glared at one another for a few moments.

For a second, Elizabeth wondered if he was about to pick her up and bundle her into the carriage forcibly. He seemed quite capable of it.

But he did not.

Finally, it was Mr. Darcy who broke the silence.

"Miss Bennet. Please. If I cannot appeal to your sense of logic and self-preservation, will you at least consider the feelings of your eldest sister? How would Mrs. Bingley feel if her beloved Elizabeth were to be banished to her chamber for Twelfth Night, missing the Netherfield ball altogether, due to a terrible case of winter chill?"

Elizabeth sighed. It was no good. He had

found her weak spot, and had exploited it mercilessly. Fear of upsetting Jane drove her to accept his offer.

She put one reluctant dripping foot in front of the other until she was near enough to touch the carriage. Her boots squelched as she stepped onto the footboard. Mr. Darcy held the door still so that she could climb aboard.

Miss Bingley shrank back on the seat and moved her skirts aside.

"Girls," she said to Miss Darcy and Miss Carrington, "please move over and sit here, next to me. Then Miss Bennet can have the other seat to herself."

They did as they were told, and Elizabeth sat on the vacant seat, fuming to herself. All four ladies crammed themselves onto one side of the carriage, while Miss Bennet was left on the other, burning with embarrassment.

The driver jumped down and slammed shut the door. Elizabeth felt the carriage rock as he climbed back up to the driving seat. Then there was a second lurch, as Mr. Darcy climbed up alongside him.

That was exactly what Elizabeth wanted to avoid. Now Mr. Darcy, in all his finery, would be soaked to the skin, and she would be responsible.

As well as this, she was making Mr. Bingley's nice new carriage into a mud-bath, and causing four other ladies to suffer a cramped journey back to Netherfield.

She had no choice, however. Mr. Darcy had made it clear he was not going to take no for an answer.

Elizabeth turned her face to the window and willed the journey back to Longbourn to be as short as possible.

AT LAST, the carriage arrived at Longbourn. Elizabeth was very glad to be at home once more.

The door opened, ready for Elizabeth to disembark. But it was not the driver who held it open. Instead, a soaking wet Mr. Darcy unfastened the latch, and offered assistance in getting Elizabeth down from the steps. She took his hand, and descended to the ground.

The sight of Mr. Darcy in wet clothing made her catch her breath. It had been expected, of course, but the visual impact was quite something. He had pushed his dark hair back a little way from his face, presumably to keep the rivulets of water out of his eyes. His jacket had grown dark with the dampness too, and clung to his torso. Altogether, he had the appearance of somebody who had jumped into a river for a prank.

"Mr. Darcy..." Elizabeth began, but she could not finish the sentence. She felt her cheeks burning, and forced herself to look away. If she looked at him for a moment longer, she would find herself quite unable to formulate a sentence.

"Miss Bennet," Mr. Darcy began. But he did not finish his sentence either.

It was then that Elizabeth realised he was still holding her hand.

She drew it away at once, taking care to look at the ground and not meet his eye. Looking into his eyes seemed to render her quite foolish, and that would not do at all.

By this time, the front door had opened. One of the Bennets' footmen came out to meet them, followed by Kitty, who shrieked when she saw the state of Elizabeth.

"Oh, good grief!" Kitty yelled. "What on earth

has happened to you two? You look like half-drowned weasels!"

"It is raining, Kitty," Elizabeth said, dryly. "Astonishingly, we find ourselves covered in the aforementioned rain. Is that not extraordinary?"

"Very funny. Is the carriage leaking?"

"No. I was... walking."

"And Mr. Darcy was walking alone with you?" Kitty looked scandalised.

"No, of course he was not. Kitty, would you mind taking these new gloves to my maid, and letting her know that I shall need her attention shortly?" Elizabeth handed the sodden paper parcel to Kitty.

Kitty did as she was asked, chuckling to herself about Elizabeth's ruined bonnet.

Mr. Darcy gave a short bow. "If you have everything you need, Miss Bennet, I must return my sister to Netherfield."

"Of course." Elizabeth curtsied, feeling her cheeks warming again. "I am most obliged to you for your kindness in bringing me home, Mr. Darcy."

"Please, do not mention it. It is only a pity that I could not persuade you to accept a ride before you were caught in the rain, and not afterwards. Since you were inevitably bound to agree with me in the end, it would have been far better to have done so from the beginning."

Elizabeth narrowed her eyes at him. He frowned back at her.

What a condescending man he was. Any gratitude she had felt evaporated on contact with his pompous, superior tone of voice.

He had known she would agree in the end? How arrogant.

If only she had found a way to refuse his earlier offer of the first Twelfth Night dance! But there had been none. Now she could not help but slightly dread the ball, when previously she had been looking forward to it.

But this was not the time for self-pity. Now that Jane was with child, Elizabeth would need to ensure she was as helpful as possible to her sister, in the management of this and all other matters. She resolved to do her sisterly duty, and throw herself into the festivities with her usual enthusiasm. Any less would mean letting down her beloved Jane.

She said goodbye to the three ladies in the carriage, and promised to see them all at the ball. Miss Bingley attempted to make a half-comical, half-pointed remark about the wet muddy mess on the floor of the carriage, but Elizabeth pretended she had not heard, and made her way to her own front door.

When it closed behind her, and she was surrounded by her own four walls, she could finally relax. Leaning against the heavy oak panelling, she let out a huge sigh of relief.

"Let's get you out of these wet things, ma'am," her maid said, and Elizabeth followed her thankfully up the stairs.

CHAPTER 15

Elizabeth submitted to preparations for the ball, allowing her maid to unravel her hair into perfect curls. She was a little tense, but resisted the feeling with all her might.

As far as her father was concerned, she knew there was less to be worried about that day than there had been a few days previously. Mr. Bennet was able to get up daily now, and the doctor was content with his progress.

Mrs. Bennet had also resumed her usual activities. Apart from regular explosions of frustration at Lydia's absence, she was in reasonably good spirits too.

However, to their dismay, Lydia had still not returned. Nor had she sent any direct correspondence to explain where she was. To their relief,

Kitty had met a mutual friend while shopping in Meryton, who had news of Lydia. She had received a letter from Lydia's friend, the draper's daughter. The letter had said that Lydia and the draper's daughter were having a gay time at one of the friends' aunts' lodgings by the sea at Weymouth, and that they would return presently.

Though she was pleased to learn that Lydia was not in any trouble, Elizabeth had not been greatly reassured by this account. She knew Weymouth was considered a less than respectable place to visit, particularly for a girl of Lydia's age. They did not know the friend's family at all, and could not vouch for their respectability. But at least it provided some measure of certainty that Lydia was safe and well, and in the company of an adult female. In that, Elizabeth found some comfort, as did her mother, Mary and Kitty.

"I wish Mary were not coming with us this evening, Lizzy," grumbled Kitty, as the maid slipped on Kitty's final layer of clothing. "She insists upon giving perfect strangers improving lectures about all sorts of tiresome subjects, and she does not know when to hold her tongue. She is the worst possible company." Kitty winced as her maid drew in the strings of her stays. "And if she sits down at the pianoforte, I shall quite possibly tear her away myself. And then I shall push her down a well."

"Hold your tongue, Kitty. You shall do nothing of the sort." Mrs. Bennet cuffed the top of Kitty's head with her palm as she breezed in. Her maid readjusted Kitty's hair patiently.

"And I shall push Lydia down the well next, for leaving me to go to the ball with Mary."

Mrs. Bennet snorted at her. "That's *enough*. When your sister comes home, you may leave her to me. I shall make my view of her shenanigans quite clear. Oh, yes! You need have no fear on that score. Until then, let us go about our business like sensible ladies."

Kitty sighed theatrically. "Yes, Mamma."

Elizabeth looked down at her white gown. It was a little low-cut on the bodice for her taste, but she had to admit it was very suitable for a grand ball. The skirt flowed beautifully as she spun around. It had been made for a night of dancing.

She slipped on her new gloves, pulling them over her elbows and smoothing out the wrinkles at the wrist. Though the rain had destroyed their packaging, the gloves themselves had been undamaged by the water. That was lucky.

She admired them, turning her arms this way and that. Definitely a good purchase, she told herself, even if the excursion to Meryton was not quite the peaceful daydream-filled occasion she had hoped.

Who would ask her to dance at the ball that night? She wondered which gentlemen had been invited, and whether she would know many of them. They would not all be gentlemen from the immediate vicinity, that was certain. Some would be coming from the surrounding areas. Perhaps some might hail from even further afield. Elizabeth wished she had looked through the guest list with Jane before leaving Netherfield so hastily two days ago.

Of course, Elizabeth had to dance with the impossible Mr. Darcy first. There was no getting away from that. But then she would be free to dance with others, and she hoped there might be enough genial gentlemen to go around. At the public balls in Meryton, there was frequently a surfeit of ladies, and that meant many were left sitting around idly for hours, hoping to be asked.

A more even ratio of gentlemen to ladies would be better. Elizabeth felt sure that Mr. Bingley would have enough gentleman friends for Jane to invite, and they might all therefore be more certain of a good evening's dancing.

"The carriage is ready," called Mary. "Come on, everyone."

"You go on ahead, Mother," said Elizabeth. "I shall just attend to Father for a moment, to make sure all is well."

Mr. Bennet was in the library, with a footman in attendance. He was reading, as always, and nursed a cup of hot milk in one hand.

"Well, now. Don't you look regal, Lizzy dear? I had no idea that was you, at first. I thought Princess Sophia had come to call."

Elizabeth smiled. She sat on the footstool at her father's knee.

"Why, thank you, Father. We shall miss you this evening. Is there anything you would like me to do before we go? I have left instructions with the steward to send word to Netherfield immediately if you have need of us."

"Oh, balderdash. Be off with you," Mr. Bennet said, shooing Lizzy away with his open book. "Go on. Leave an old man to his reading. Go forth, and make merry. No doubt you shall all tell me about it tomorrow, at *great* length." His wry face made Elizabeth laugh.

"Very well. Have a peaceful evening with your book. Be sure to sleep well, and we shall see you in the morning." She kissed him and nodded to the footman, who bowed.

In the hallway, she turned obediently as her maid wrapped her in a travelling cloak. Her mother and sisters were already in the carriage. One of the horses whinnied impatiently.

"Do come *on*, Lizzy, for heaven's sake," Kitty called.

"Coming," Elizabeth said, lifting her skirts as she crossed the threshold.

Upon sitting down in the carriage, a pang of nerves hit Elizabeth in the very centre of her stomach. She took a deep, calming breath, and forced herself to smile at her family. Scolding herself for her silly feelings, she concentrated on breathing slowly and evenly.

The evening would be enjoyable, and they would all dance, and make merry, and that would be that. There was really no need for agitation of this kind.

"Are you quite all right, dear?" Her mother

peered at her from the other seat. "Your cheeks have turned rosy."

"Yes, quite all right, Mother." The feeling subsided, and Elizabeth concentrated on her sisters' animated conversation instead. They were still bickering about who would be asked to dance first, and Elizabeth could not help but smile at their youthful vigour. Though she was only one-and-twenty, she sometimes felt older. Since Jane left, she had often felt as though she was the main adult in the family. It wore her down, though she ignored it.

But tonight would be different. Tonight, she would dance, and make merry, and laugh with her family and friends. Tonight would be a night to remember.

The carriage door slammed shut, the driver nudged the horses, and they were on their way.

CHAPTER 16

Netherfield was already thronging with people when they arrived. Their carriage had to wait behind two earlier arrivals, and Kitty's excitement was plain.

"Lizzy! Is that the Duke and Duchess of Marlborough?"

Elizabeth peered out of the carriage window, but it was fogged with steam and the light outside was too dim for her to make out any faces. "I cannot say, Kitty."

"We shall see many fine guests tonight, and many handsome gentlemen, and we must try to pace ourselves accordingly," said Mary, in a grave tone. "Otherwise, Kitty, you in particular shall burn out too fast, like a candle with two wicks."

"Oh hush, Mary. Some of us like to enjoy life. We're not all plodding dullards."

"Girls, girls. Stop your quarrelling." Mrs. Bennet adjusted her jacket and beamed at them all. "This is most thrilling, is it not? So many fine gentlemen and ladies. And hasn't our Jane done a splendid job? Look at that greenery!"

As they stepped down from the coach, the full effect of the Twelfth Night decorations hit them. Mistletoe and holly bedecked the doorway, in a most pleasing manner. Inside the grand hall, ribbon-tied sprigs of seasonal ivy and holly were pinned to the walls, while bunches of mistletoe hung down from the tops of doorways.

"Careful not to be accosted by anybody unsuitable when you stand under there," Mrs. Bennet exclaimed to her three daughters. "Before standing under mistletoe, *always* be sure that there is nobody around whom you would not care to kiss. Gentlemen can be quite free with their kisses on Twelfth Night, and it would not do to be compromised."

"We shall remain vigilant at all times." Elizabeth gave her mother a solemn look, then laughed. "But do not worry, Mother. We shall not find ourselves stuck in the company of men we do not like. We are nimble, and shall escape long before they can trap us."

"Yes, Mamma," agreed Kitty. "We are hounds among elephants."

"Hmm." Mrs. Bennet turned to allow a maid to remove her travelling layers. "And here is Jane, to greet us. Jane, my dearest girl!"

Jane was indeed waiting in the greeting line, along with Mrs. Hurst, and Miss Bingley. She curtseyed at her family and smiled warmly at Elizabeth.

"The house looks wonderful," Lizzy whispered, as she took her sister's hands. "You see? You did not need any help at all."

"I did receive quite a lot of *help*," Jane whispered back, gesturing subtly with her eyes at Mr. Bingley's sisters. "We are now casting lots at the door to see who will spend the evening with whom. Ladies must take a name and be allocated to a gentleman for the entire evening. Miss Bingley suggested it at dinner when you were here, do you remember? It is quite the fashion in London, I am told. Later in the evening, we must also take character cards, and spend the remainder of the evening as a couple in character. That was an innovation by Mrs. Hurst."

"Oh, good Lord," Kitty said. "If I get landed with Mr. Collins and have to play the character of Besotted Bride, I shall immediately go home."

Jane laughed. "Let us hope no such bad luck befalls you."

After greeting the rest of the host party, they all made their way to the ballroom. Two identical handsome footmen bowed. They each held a basket, filled with small folds of paper.

"Good evening, ma'am," one said to Mrs. Bennet. He held aloft his basket, for her to choose a paper fold.

"Gracious!" Mrs. Bennet shrieked at the footmen. "Are you twins? I daresay even your own mother could not tell you apart!" She helped herself to a slip of paper.

"We are twins, ma'am," confirmed the second.

Mary went to take a slip of paper from his basket but he shook his head. "Ma'am, this is the character basket, to be dipped into after the feast. Please take a name slip from my brother for the time being."

They all took slips of paper and walked into the main room. The soft candlelight gave it a warm glow, and the space was already three-quarters full. Elizabeth took out her fan. It was going to be a hot evening among the crowd, despite the cold weather outside.

Kitty was almost hopping up and down with joy. "Should we open the names now?"

"In a moment." Elizabeth enjoyed the moment of not yet knowing to whom she was allocated. She scanned the room for a clue. Would it be the tall auburn-haired soldier in the red coat, talking to an elderly lady? Would it be the man with corn-coloured hair and a fetching dark suit? Or would it be the dreaded Mr. Collins, their cousin? She spotted him in the corner, with his wife. Elizabeth waved at Mrs. Collins, who left her husband's side and came over.

"Elizabeth! So glad you could come."

"It is wonderful to see you, Charlotte. How are you and Mr. Collins?"

A smile flickered for a second on Mrs. Collins' face. She leaned in and spoke to Elizabeth in a soft voice.

"Mr. Collins spends much time at Rosings, with his patron, Lady Catherine de Bourgh. I find that between my domestic activities, and his commitments to his patron, we are able to see each other only fleetingly. This arrangement has proved agreeable to all parties."

Her eyes crinkled as she smiled at Elizabeth.

"I am so glad to hear married life suits you, Charlotte, my dear friend. Have you drawn lots?"

"Yes, and we have yet to open our slips. Have you yet discovered the name in yours?"

"Not yet. I am relishing the moment of uncertainty, in case I find out the name within is somebody disagreeable."

"You never know. It could be your future husband."

They both laughed.

"The odds are very much against it," Elizabeth said, "regrettable though that may be. But come. Let us open our slips all together."

Mrs. Collins beckoned over her husband, and he greeted his cousins and Mrs. Bennet in his usual fashion, with a bow that was much too deep, and too prolonged.

"It is my great honour, Mrs. Bennet, to—"

"Let us open the papers, Mr. Collins," interrupted Mrs. Bennet sharply. "We have waited long enough. You can regale us all with niceties afterwards."

Elizabeth began to unfold her name slip,

which took longer than expected due to her gloves. They had not yet worn in, and were still somewhat stiff.

Kitty snorted. "Oh, bother. I've got Colonel Grayson."

Mrs. Bennet hooted with laughter. "Mr. Hurst for me. Well, I never."

"I'm with Mr. Richard Caversham," said Mary. "Does anyone know him? I've never met him before. Hope he's dashing."

Mrs. Collins held up her piece of paper. "My slip says Mr. George Lowborough. Is that the gentleman talking to Colonel Grayson now?"

Mrs. Bennet followed Mrs. Collins's gaze. "Yes, that's the one. Lovely fellow. Brother is an officer in the army, I understand."

Kitty nudged Elizabeth in the ribs. "Who have you got, Lizzy?"

She smoothed out the paper and stared at the neat handwriting within.

Blood seemed to drain from her head and she felt dizzy. Voices clamoured around her, but she was frozen to the spot.

"Lizzy? Why do you not speak, girl?"

"Miss Bennet, are you quite well?"

"Is everything all right, Elizabeth?"

Elizabeth looked up at them all, and then back down to the paper, willing it to be different the second time she looked at it. But, of course, it was not.

The slip read "Mr. Fitzwilliam Darcy".

"Oh *dear*," she muttered.

CHAPTER 17

"Well, go and tell him, for pity's sake!" Mrs. Bennet gave Elizabeth a little shove in the direction of Mr. Darcy, who was conversing with Mr. Bingley and Miss Bingley in the corner.

"Already?" groaned Elizabeth. "I am already promised to him for the first dance. May I not enjoy a few moments to survey the room on my own first?"

"No you may not," her mother scolded. "That is not how the game works, Lizzy. We are all going to find our allocated partners now. You cannot stand on your own, like a lost duckling. I insist on your joining Mr. Darcy this very instant."

It was too late anyway. Kitty had scampered

over to him already and was speaking animat-edly to him. He looked impatiently down at Kitty at first, as though wondering what on earth she was talking about. Then he looked up.

He was searching the room for her, Elizabeth knew. There was nothing else for it. She was going to have to walk over to him.

"Mr. Darcy," she said, bobbing into a quick curtsey. She held up her unfolded paper slip. "I am afraid we are partners this evening." Before he could respond, she cut in again. "I shall not protest if you wish to dance with other ladies, however. Whenever you wish to ask another to dance, I beseech you to please feel free. Enjoy yourself as you usually would."

"Miss Bennet," he replied, bowing. "Thank you for making such a magnanimous offer. However, I see no need to alter the arrangement laid out for us by our hosts. For that reason, I feel it unnecessary to agree an alternative code of conduct, for either of us. Your views are, of course, noted."

Elizabeth rolled her eyes heavenward as he turned back to his friends to excuse himself. So he was effectively telling her she could not dance with anyone else either. The nerve of the man.

Having notified his friends of his new temporary partnership, Mr. Darcy took Elizabeth's arm and led her to the centre of the room, where dancing was about to start. The musicians had taken their positions and were sounding a few preliminary notes.

Elizabeth looked her partner up and down as they faced one another. He stood tall and ramrod-straight, his eyes focused some distance away over her head, with a stern expression on his face.

She wondered if he ever relaxed. Perhaps he only did so in the company of his own upper-class kind, and not among second-rate country folk like them.

"Do you enjoy dancing, Mr. Darcy?"

He glanced very briefly at her face, then away again. "Not particularly."

"Gracious. Then I cannot imagine why you asked me to dance two whole days ago."

"You find my request a strange one?"

"One might reasonably assume a man is very fond of dancing, if he chooses to secure a partner days in advance."

"One might reasonably assume dancing is required at a ball. Therefore it is quite within the bounds of expected behaviour to secure a partner for the first set. By my calculation, this may be done at any point before the dance begins. There is nothing untoward about doing so during the preceding week."

Elizabeth shifted from foot to foot, trying to push down the tide of annoyance which was rising in her. She stood in the line of ladies, awaiting the opening bars of music. Mr. Darcy was directly opposite her in the line of gentle-men. He was by far the tallest in the row, flanked as he was on his left by an older gentleman with white whiskers, and on his right by a slender, awkward-looking youth of no more than around nineteen.

"How old are you, Mr. Darcy?"

He looked at her, as though this was an unex-pected question. "Eight-and-twenty. Why do you ask?"

"Merely curiosity."

"I see. How old are you?"

"It is not polite to ask a lady's age, you know."

"But it is polite to ask a gentleman's?"

"It is not impolite."

Mr. Darcy glared at her. "Thank you for educating me on this distinction."

"But I will tell you my age anyway. I am one-and-twenty, which I have reason to understand is terribly old."

"For a horse, perhaps. Not for a lady."

Elizabeth could not help but giggle at this.

The dance began, and they moved around the other couples, turning and changing direction as the dance required. Mr. Darcy was an elegant dancer, and kept time perfectly. When the white-haired gentleman to his left stepped out of time, Mr. Darcy stepped aside neatly and avoided a collision.

For the first few minutes, neither of them said a word. Elizabeth disliked this. She found silent dancing most uncivilised, and resolved to restart the conversation somehow.

After racking her brain to think of an unproblematic topic, she decided on Netherfield itself.

"How do you find Netherfield, Mr. Darcy?" she said,

"It is a fine house, populated by a fine couple."

Elizabeth nodded. She was pleased he seemed to like her sister. "You must have known Mrs. Hurst and Miss Bingley for a long time?"

"Yes."

"What do you think of their friend, Miss Carrington?"

Mr. Darcy said nothing for a moment. Elizabeth twirled around him, and they stepped forward in unison. The couple next to them intermingled with them and circled around.

"I do not think of Miss Carrington at all."

"But you are sharing a house with her at present."

Mr. Darcy remained stony-faced. "That is true."

"Do you not have an opinion on her character, or her wit? I found it hard to prompt her to talk, but I imagine it would be easier for those staying in the same accommodation for several days."

"I doubt that I shall ever have much of a conversation with Miss Carrington." He seemed thoroughly bored by the idea. "Perhaps you might more easily find the answers to your questions if you addressed Miss Carrington directly."

Could Mr. Darcy really be so miserly with his time that he did not even bother to talk to his fellow houseguests? It seemed awfully rude to Elizabeth. Perhaps she just did not know the ways of the rich.

"Do you feel it difficult to talk to her because she is so very shy? Or is there another reason?"

Mr. Darcy turned Elizabeth around and led her back to their starting position. They waited while the other couples turned circles down the centre of the parallel lines of dancers. Then they began to dance with the other members of the dance, one by one.

When they returned to one another's sides, Mr. Darcy addressed Elizabeth again. "Is there a reason why you are so concerned with Miss Carrington?"

"Not at all. I merely wish to make out her character. And, I suppose, yours. The two of you are like closed books to the casual observer. You have that trait in common."

His face was a sculpted rock now, and still unreadable.

"There is no great merit in throwing one's character open to the casual observer." With a flourish, he turned to step around her, and took her hand again. "Perhaps Miss Carrington feels similarly."

"Perhaps." Elizabeth mirrored his moves, circling him and returning to her starting spot.

The atmosphere between them was distinctly

chilly, despite the sweltering heat in the ball-room. Elizabeth felt agitated. She was not expressing herself quite as she wanted to. Something about Mr. Darcy's presence threw her off-balance.

In fact, Mr. Darcy's proximity had an effect on her that she would rather not think about. When his eyes alighted on hers, they seemed to transmit a warmth to her cheeks which was quite at odds with the frosty nature of his personality. She did not know what to make of this. He seemed to have very little interest in anybody outside his circle, and she could not see why he would be feeling any warmth towards her.

She also knew, deep down, that she was not enquiring after his feelings quite so innocently as she had pretended. Miss Bingley had insisted that Mr. Darcy and Miss Carrington would soon be a couple. It was like an itch from which Elizabeth could not rid herself.

Did he genuinely have feelings for this quiet young lady, or not? Why was it that she felt she simply must know?

And why should it bother her, either way? She could not even answer herself on that score.

They had at least another fifteen minutes left of this dance, and she would be tied to Mr. Darcy's side for much of the remainder of the evening. That ridiculous scheme of casting lots at the door! If only Jane had held firm and refused to indulge her sisters-in-law with their madcap ideas. But Jane had been amenable and sweet about it, and that was just like Jane.

Elizabeth resolved to endure the dance without complaint. Then she might be asked to dance by somebody else. Several gentlemen looked admiringly in her direction as she danced with Mr. Darcy. She felt hopeful that another man might step in at some stage.

Perhaps Mr. Darcy did not mean what he said about ruling out other dances? After all, he himself may grow tired, or wish to converse with other guests. Would that mean she would be sitting as a wallflower while the rest of the party danced? She rather hoped not.

Surely he would not object to her dancing with another guest, in that instance? Dancing was a most enjoyable pastime. She relished the opportunity to do so whenever it occurred.

It did not escape her attention that Mr. Darcy also seemed to be attracting appreciative looks.

She could see little clusters of ladies collected around the dancing space, watching him, and whispering to one another. He must have been one of the most eligible bachelors in the room, so it was not surprising.

Elizabeth smiled to herself, thinking how they must all be hoping he would ask them to dance next. They probably hoped he would fall in love with them too, and whisk them away to his Derbyshire estate. Poor, deluded optimists. Men like Mr. Darcy did not fall in love with country girls at a ball.

She could simplify that sentiment further. Men like Mr. Darcy did not fall in love. He said so himself, more or less. His heart was a block of ice that would never melt.

"Is something amusing you, Miss Bennet?"

She looked up to meet her partner's eyes, and realised she was still smiling to herself. "No. My apologies; I was miles away. Please excuse me."

The music began to draw to a close, and they moved apart. Mr. Darcy bowed graciously. Elizabeth curtseyed.

"Would you care to sit down?"

Mr. Darcy held out his arm to Elizabeth. She was on the verge of refusing, but then thought better of it. She would do as he asked to begin with, and hope that he tired of her before long, so that she might dance with other people.

Mr. Darcy's arm was strong and firm, as Elizabeth took it. He led her to a bank of chairs, and a dozen envious female eyes followed them all the way.

"Let us sit," he said, and planted himself next to her.

CHAPTER 18

The room really was becoming uncomfortably hot. Elizabeth waved her fan all around her neckline, adoring the feeling of cool air on her skin.

It appeared that Mr. Darcy was about to address her again, when Mrs. Hurst and Miss Bingley sidled up to them.

"Oh, for pity's sake, somebody get me out of here." Miss Bingley screwed up her face, as though she had just tasted something disagreeable. "If I have to dance with that buffoon again, I shall break my own ankle just to alleviate the horror."

"Goodness, you sound gloomy, Miss Bingley. Who is your partner this evening?" Elizabeth asked, trying to work out the nature of Miss Bingley's predicament.

"That dreaded clergyman. Ghastly chap."

"Mr. Collins?"

"That's the fellow."

"Mr. Collins is our cousin," Elizabeth said, with a small smile.

Miss Bingley was momentarily speechless. Mr. Darcy glared at her.

"Oh. Well, I…" She seemed to be having difficulty finishing her sentence. Elizabeth understood Miss Bingley's reluctance to repeat her views in front of Elizabeth now she knew of the family connection. She almost felt sorry for her. Mr. Collins certainly could be taxing company, after all.

"Miss Bingley, I had no idea you and that… *gentleman* were related," Mrs. Hurst said, with an icy smile. "Please accept my heartfelt apologies for such a tactless remark."

"Please think nothing of it."

It was only then that Elizabeth noticed Miss Carrington skulking behind the two sisters. She looked miserable again. Elizabeth felt sorry for her most of all. It appeared that Miss Bingley was largely ignoring her, and Mrs. Hurst was following suit. Yet they were still dragging the poor young lady around after them. Why on earth had they brought Miss Carrington here, if they weren't even going to talk to her?

"Who is your partner today, Miss Carrington?"

She looked at Elizabeth regretfully. "My slip of paper said Mr. Bingley."

Elizabeth looked around, confused. "Then where is he?"

"Miss Bingley told him I needed to be released from the game, so that I might find an unmarried man to talk to." Miss Carrington looked rather disappointed by this state of events, but said no more.

"That's not really in the spirit of the thing, Miss Bingley," Mr. Darcy said.

"Oh, come now, Mr. Darcy. It is all very well for Charles to dance with Miss Carrington all night. He has already secured himself a bride, and a happy marriage. But Miss Carrington has been most grievously injured by love, and needs urgently to find a gentleman who is more suitable. Dancing with a married man will not fulfil that requirement."

Miss Carrington was by now bright red, and

looking as though she would rather disappear into a crack in the floor.

"I am sorry to hear that," Elizabeth said. She hoped Miss Bingley would be more discreet, as Miss Carrington gave every impression of wanting her to be quiet.

Unfortunately, Miss Bingley did not take the hint.

"Yes, terrible business. You see, poor Miss Carrington has had a very difficult twelve months. In the summer, she accepted a proposal. But she was moved to rescind her acceptance a few weeks before the wedding. Embarrassing, to say the least. If she does not find herself a replacement fiancé soon, I fear Miss Carrington will find herself forever tainted by that act of untimely rejection. People will consider her an untrustworthy match."

Miss Carrington had tears in her eyes now. It seemed that Miss Bingley was in full flow. Elizabeth racked her brain to find something to say that would change the subject.

"Well, my aunt Gardiner always says—" Elizabeth began.

Miss Bingley cut in across Elizabeth, as though she had not spoken. "It is most destructive of a woman's reputation to be seen to reverse her favour like that. Sympathy may be won by the gentleman, but sympathy does not extend to the lady. Miss Carrington needs to show herself to be a woman capable of returning a man's honestly-given attentions. Otherwise, she may as well give up now, and resign herself to a life of genteel poverty and misery."

"Goodness," said Mrs. Hurst, "I don't suppose *you'd* care to swap with Miss Carrington, would you Miss Bennet?"

Elizabeth stared at her. "You want me to take Mr. Bingley as my partner and pass on Mr. Darcy to Miss Carrington?" This rankled with her. She had been annoyed about having been partnered with Mr. Darcy in the first place, but something inside her resisted the swap.

"Yes. Mr. Darcy is unmarried, after all. Perhaps he might like to spend some time with a single lady such as Miss Carrington. She comes from a good family of means. They are of course far more evenly suited, if one overlooks her history of last-minute refusals."

Mrs. Hurst's jab at the Bennets' social and financial standing did not pass unnoticed. Elizabeth took a second to calm herself inside, and smiled sweetly. If the two sisters were united in their mission to pair Miss Carrington with Mr. Darcy, there was little she could do about it. She might as well resign herself to it, and make the best of the situation. In any case, she would enjoy her brother-in-law's company very much.

They would find it difficult to achieve their aim if they continued speaking of Miss Carrington's broken engagement, however. That would hardly win a gentleman's trust. Elizabeth reflected on this. Why were they at pains to stress Miss Carringtons' faults, if they wished to set her up with Mr. Darcy? She began to understand that their motives may in fact be a little more obscure than she had first thought.

It was all too complicated and silly to dwell on much longer. She smiled brightly at them all.

"If Mr. Darcy agrees to the exchange, I should be happy to swap him for Mr. Bingley. Anybody would have an enjoyable evening in Mr. Bingley's amiable company, and I shall see plenty of my sister while talking to her husband. So that will do very well."

"Marvellous. That's settled, then." Mrs. Hurst clapped her hands.

"No, it is not." Mr. Darcy's dark eyes flashed.

"I will not condone the dismantling of Mrs. Bingley's game. Need I remind you, Mrs. Hurst, that the lottery was your sister's idea? You both spent an inordinate amount of time convincing your hostess to indulge your whims. The least you can do is respect the outcome. The original arrangements stand."

"Are you saying you do not wish to spend time with Miss Carrington?"

Miss Carrington looked crushed by what Miss Bingley was saying. With a little yelp of distress, she rushed from the room. Elizabeth saw her sister Jane go after her.

Elizabeth was shocked at Miss Bingley's rudeness.

Mr. Darcy's face was thunderous. "Do not put words into my mouth, Miss Bingley. I am saying that if you remove the element of randomness, you may as well not participate at all. We are all guests in Mr. Bingley's house, and we have agreed to abide by the festive games of the night. It would be disrespectful in the extreme to customise them, thereby destroying the entire plan."

Mrs. Hurst and Miss Bingley looked at one another sourly, then looked at Elizabeth.

Elizabeth shrugged. There was nothing she could do, if her partner did not agree to waive the agreement.

Secretly, she was rather pleased that he would not give into the two sisters' manipulative games. Although it did mean that she was definitely stuck with him for the entire night.

Why didn't that dismay her? Why didn't the idea of being with the disagreeable man ruin her night?

Why did she feel a little burst of joy, deep in her heart?

She pushed the thought aside as soon as it arrived.

At that moment, Mary appeared at Elizabeth's elbow. "Are you enjoying yourself, Lizzy? Mr. Caversham here is a fine dancer. He wished to be introduced to you, so here we are. Mr. Caversham, may I present my sister, Miss Bennet?"

Elizabeth curtseyed to the handsome man at her sister's side. He bowed deeply, with a smile on his face.

"It is an honour to meet you, Miss Bennet. I feel I already know you, from dancing with your sister for the previous set. She speaks highly of you."

Elizabeth could not imagine Mary spending much time speaking of any of her sisters, highly or otherwise, but she was pleased to meet this new gentleman. Mr. Caversham was even better-looking when he spoke. His eyes shone and lit up his face when he smiled, and he had a slightly mischievous angle to his smile, which she found charming.

"Thank you, Mr. Caversham. Do you come from Meryton?"

"No, I hail from Winchester, in Hampshire. I am here in Hertfordshire only for the evening. But if the ladies of Hertfordshire are all as fetching as the ones I have met tonight, I fear I am living in the wrong part of the country altogether."

Mrs. Hurst and Miss Bingley laughed gracefully. Mr. Darcy looked away, disgustedly.

Elizabeth smiled at him. "You flatter us, Mr. Caversham."

She could not help but notice that he was looking at her most of all. She glanced at her partner. Mr. Darcy's face was set in its usual proud expression, surveying the rest of the room, but keeping a discreet watch on this new interloper.

Mr. Caversham bowed once more. "Not at all, Miss Bennet. In fact, would you do me the honour of dancing with me for the next set? That is, if I can prise you away from your partner."

"Thank you, but I would not want to leave Mary without a dance partner," Elizabeth said quickly.

"Oh, good grief, please don't worry about that." Mary fanned herself and exhaled loudly. "I'm looking forward to a little rest. Mother is over there, so I will sit with her for a little while. Please, go ahead."

"There we are, then." Mr. Caversham's face lit up with a smile. "Nobody can possibly object."

Elizabeth looked at Mr. Darcy, whose face was stormy. There was no possibility of his agreeing to dance with other people. He had already made it clear that the rules of Jane's partner allocation had to be abided by.

Still, she had to ask, and he could refuse Mr. Caversham himself if he must. At least she wouldn't be the one to look rude.

"Would you excuse me for the next dance, Mr. Darcy?"

Mr. Darcy looked as if he were about to say something sharp. But then he held Elizabeth's gaze for a few seconds. She held her breath, for his gaze seemed to knock it out of her.

Instead of refusing, as she had predicted, he bowed and stepped back.

Why had he agreed?

Astonished, Elizabeth allowed Mr. Caversham to lead her to the centre of the room. She looked back over her shoulder to see Mr. Darcy's eyes searing into them as they walked.

As they started to turn about the room, Elizabeth could not help but glance back again at her partner, Mr. Darcy. Now he had stopped watching them. She caught a glimpse of him talking to Miss Bingley and Mrs. Hurst. Miss Carrington had not returned, and Elizabeth supposed that Jane had taken her elsewhere to calm down.

What a miserable time Miss Carrington must be having. Elizabeth resolved to find her again and make friends properly when the dance ended.

As she turned before Mr. Caversham, Elizabeth was surprised to notice Mr. Darcy walking towards the dance floor. Even more surprising was the fact that he was holding Miss Bingley's hand, presumably to take her to dance.

To her astonishment, Elizabeth found this peeved her slightly, though there was no good reason for it. She had precisely no right to form an opinion on Mr. Darcy's dance partners. Indeed, dancing with other people had been her idea in the first place. Of course he would dance with Miss Bingley. He had known her since childhood. There was nothing untoward in that at all.

Mr. Darcy and Miss Bingley took up their places at the end of the line, several couples away from her, and did not look in Elizabeth's direction. She turned her attention back to Mr. Caversham, who smiled broadly at her. He really was a most fine-looking gentleman.

She and Mr. Caversham continued with their dance, and when Mr Caversham spoke to her once more, she resolved to devote all her attention to him for the duration of the dance, and not divert it to anyone else in the room. After all, that was the polite thing to do.

Besides, Mr. Caversham was really very engaging and agreeable, as well as handsome. It would be no hardship for any person to spend time in his company.

The dance progressed, and the ladies skipped down in a central line while the gentleman waited aside. As she passed him, Elizabeth caught the eye of Mr. Darcy. His face was as enigmatic as ever, and she could not read his expression.

"Are you having a good time, Mr. Darcy?"

"Are you, Miss Bennet?"

Though she tried to reply, she found she could form no sensible answer for him.

When the ladies passed back the other way, she found herself longing to dance with him again, and not Mr. Caversham.

She reprimanded herself silently, but it was no use. Whatever else she felt about the disagreeable Mr. Darcy, something drew her to him. It was quite hopeless to pretend otherwise.

The thought made her quite cross with herself. But there was nothing to be done about it, other than distract herself wherever possible.

CHAPTER 19

"What a terribly dreary little ball," Miss Bingley said as they turned about the floor, with a sneer on her face.

"I am sorry you feel that way," Darcy replied. He had known Miss Bingley many years, as Bingley's youngest sister. Since the moment Bingley had rented Netherfield, Miss Bingley had made a whole lot of fuss about how miserable she was in Hertfordshire. At all times, she made sure nobody was in any doubt about her superiority. It was rather tiresome.

"Surely *you* cannot be enjoying it, Mr. Darcy?"

"I rarely enjoy events of this nature, in any location."

Miss Bingley laughed, in an affected way.

"Oh, but Mr. Darcy! You must enjoy the society balls in London, surely?"

"Not particularly."

"Do you not enjoy seeing all the beautiful young society ladies in their finery?"

Darcy refused to be drawn on this. Miss Bingley would not be deterred.

"Well, *I* rather enjoy seeing the best people in all their glory, as one does in London. It reminds one just how splendid the English aristocracy really is."

The couples separated and, one pair at a time, took a turn down the centre of the room, with the other couples lining the walkway. Apparently, Miss Bingley had a great deal of conversation left in her.

"Mr. Darcy, you must be looking forward to returning to Derbyshire soon? No doubt your sister is equally eager to make her way back to the ancestral home?"

"Wherever my sister is happy, I am happy too."

"It seems that Miss Darcy has made friends with Miss Carrington, has she not?"

"Perhaps." His sister Georgiana was a sweet girl, and made friends wherever she went. He was glad she had settled well into their visit to Netherfield.

"And do you suppose that Miss Carrington will visit you at Pemberley?"

"I have given it no thought whatever."

"Of course, Miss Carrington has designs of her own to consider."

Darcy noticed that she was raising an eyebrow and winking at him as she said this.

"Do you have something in your eye, Miss Bingley?"

Miss Bingley shook her head. "Not in the least, sir. But I understand that Miss Carrington has taken quite a shine to you."

This remark was very odd to Mr. Darcy. He did not respond.

Miss Bingley persisted." You must have noticed, Mr. Darcy, have you not?"

Mr. Darcy sighed impatiently. "I have received no impression of that kind."

"Oh! Then Miss Carrington's feminine wiles are more advanced than I had imagined."

They spun around together, with another couple. All four hands met in a knot in the centre, and they turned in a clockwise fashion.

Then the couples parted, and Miss Bingley took the opportunity to continue the subject.

"Of course, it would not do for a lady to make it plain that her preference lay in the direction of any one gentleman. I rather suspect that Miss Carrington is playing her cards close to her chest."

This pointed speculation was all getting too much for Darcy. He found it impossible to keep his irritation in check.

"Miss Bingley, if I may. What in blazes are you talking about?"

"Miss Carrington! She is a woman of good means, and most certainly on the lookout for an eligible gentlemen. Of course, some say she is poor company, and an inept conversationalist. I grant that her looks may not be to the standards a gentleman might require. She has a history of untrustworthiness. And she is one of the least fashionable ladies in London. But none of that matters, when you consider the purity of her heart. That is, of course, paramount."

Darcy was beginning to wonder whether Miss Bingley was trying to encourage him to view Miss Carrington as a potential fiancée, or to discourage him altogether. He was beginning to wonder where this was all going. She seemed to have an inordinate amount to say about Miss Carrington generally, and he found it inexplicable.

It did not help that he had been watching Miss Bennett and Mr. Caversham out of the corner of his eye at all times. His attention was never entirely on the words of Miss Bingley. He had to admit that to himself, if not to Miss Bingley.

"What kind of lady appeals to you, Mr. Darcy?"

Mr Darcy was growing exceedingly tired of this conversation, but the dance had at least twenty minutes left to run.

"I am not looking for a bride, Miss Bingley. I believe I may have made that clear before."

Miss Bingley laughed again. It was another of her confected false laughs, and this time she accompanied it with an arch toss of the head.

"But you are not averse to the idea of settling down and taking your position as the head of a family?"

"It is simply not something I am considering." Darcy was beginning to regret asking Miss Bingley to dance. He had only done so because

Miss Bennet was dancing with Mr Caversham. He had wished to show Miss Bennet that there were no hard feelings if she chose to dance with another.

He was starting to wish he had just gone to find Bingley and sat down with him for a glass of brandy.

"Then I shall advise you, for your own good." Miss Bingley seemed delighted at this prospect. "Mr. Darcy, I highly recommend that you find a lady of similar social standing to yourself. You should look for somebody at ease in good company, and somebody who you can trust to run a household with the greatest flair. Somebody who is aware of the newest and most fashionable developments in polite society, and whose grooming and appearance is of a premium standard. Of course, they should also have a sense of fun, and come from a highly respectable family. Ensure that the lady is healthy, tall and slender, in order that your children may benefit from the very best parenting stock available."

Mr. Darcy snorted." You speak as though I were looking for a breeding mare."

"The integrity of the ancestral line is of vital

importance. Let us not forget the damage that can be done by introducing an inferior parent, which will drag down the entire Darcy line. Your heir must hail from a high-quality bloodline on both sides."

"What a ghastly mercenary way to look at things."

"Not at all. Marriage is a serious business."

Darcy did not hear any more, because at that moment, he saw Elizabeth smiling happily at Mr. Caversham, and Mr. Caversham laughing. He surmised that she had just told him a joke of some kind. Mr. Caversham then said something back to her, and the two of them laughed uproariously.

Darcy's fists itched. He fought a strong urge to march over there and shove Mr. Caversham out of the way. The feeling disturbed him. He knew he had no right at all to feel territorial over Miss Bennet, just because she was his partner for the evening. Yet, there it was.

They were now five couples apart, and the dance had moved to the point where they would not again be crossing one another's paths. Mr. Darcy scowled to himself, as he went through the motions of the dance with Miss Bingley.

"Are you listening, Mr. Darcy?"

Darcy's attention snapped back to his dance partner. He longed to be rude, but dispelled the urge. There was no need for a scene. The dance would be over before long, and he could remove himself then.

"My apologies, Miss Bingley. My mind was elsewhere."

Miss Bingley glanced around, and her eyes alighted on Miss Bennet and Mr. Caversham. Her eyes narrowed, and a cold, cruel look crept onto her face.

"Mr. Darcy, I–"

With a sudden squawk of pain, she fell heavily against Darcy. He caught her deftly, steering her to the edge of the dancing couples.

"What is it, Miss Bingley?"

"My ankle! I believe I may have sprained it."

Darcy placed his arm around Miss Bingley and helped her to the side of the room, pulling out a chair for her and easing her into it. He pulled another chair forward and bade her lift her leg onto it.

Grabbing a member of the waiting staff, he ordered bandages and a cold compress to be brought immediately.

"Oh really, Mr. Darcy, I do not wish to be an inconvenience." The smug smile on Miss Bingley's face suggested that she was more than happy to be inconveniencing Mr. Darcy at that moment.

"Please rest, Miss Bingley. Do not excite yourself further with conversation."

Mr. Darcy lifted Miss Bingley's foot and rested it upon a cushion to elevate her ankle further.

At that moment, Miss Bennet ran over, followed by Mr. Caversham. Darcy found, once again, that Mr. Caversham's face was astoundingly disagreeable.

"Has there been an injury? I shall inform Jane." Miss Bennet examined Miss Bingley's ankle. "There is no sign of swelling. Perhaps the damage is not as bad as you feared, Miss Bingley."

Miss Bingley winced. "Oh, I don't know about that. The pain is throbbing. I only hope I have not broken it."

Miss Bennet took hold of Miss Bingley's foot and turned it suddenly all around. Miss Bingley looked surprised, but did not cry out.

"It is not broken. You would have been in

agony then if it had been."

Mr. Darcy suppressed a smile at Miss Bennet's matter-of-fact investigations.

"I shall go and inform Mrs. Bingley myself," he said. He ignored Miss Bingley's protestations. He had no doubt at all that her injury was feigned, and he would be happy to pass her off to her sister-in-law's care.

Most importantly of all, Miss Bennet was back at his side. He would do his best to keep her there, even though he knew after tonight he would rarely, if ever, see her again.

"Please wait with the patient, Miss Bennet. I shall be back with Mrs. Bingley in a moment," Darcy said, making it plain he expected her to remain with him rather than return to Mr. Caversham.

"I shall be here," she said.

CHAPTER 20

Miss Bingley made a great show of complaining about her ankle. The way she described the accident, it may as well have snapped in two.

But Elizabeth was dubious. Not only had she seen that there was no swelling, but Miss Bingley seemed quite composed. Despite the theatrics, she seemed as calm as ever. Elizabeth felt sure a lady would behave quite differently if she were in severe pain.

"There is a doctor among our guests," Jane said, as she swept over to them. She looked quite anxious. Elizabeth squeezed her hand, and leaned over to whisper to her.

"I rather think Miss Bingley will make a miraculous recovery before the evening is out."

Jane raised her eyebrows and Elizabeth smiled.

"Surely you are not suggesting the injury is not genuine?" Jane whispered back, looking shocked.

"Oh, Jane. You are such a sweet thing. It would never cross your mind to formulate such a scheme, but that does not mean nobody else would. Rest assured, I am certain that Miss Bingley will be back on her feet just as soon as she has achieved her objective."

"And what might that be?"

"Now that is the question." Elizabeth grinned at her sister. "Who knows? But I am sure at some point we will find out."

MR. DARCY STOOD a few feet away, talking to Mr. Caversham. Elizabeth wondered what they were talking about. Certainly, Mr. Darcy's facial expression was not amiable. It seemed that he felt little patience for whatever he was hearing, or perhaps it was just that he disliked Mr. Caversham. Either way, Elizabeth could tell that Mr.

Darcy was looking forward to moving away from Mr. Caversham.

"Jane, did Mr. Darcy know Mr. Caversham previously?"

"Not to my knowledge. As I understand it, Mr. Caversham has connections with Mr. Bingley's cousins, but Mr. Darcy had never met him."

Elizabeth could not understand Mr. Darcy's apparent antipathy. Mr. Caversham had been excellent company on the dance floor. Elizabeth had not laughed so much since the last time she and Charlotte had met for a country walk, and had ruthlessly dissected their hopeless love lives. That never happened any more, since Charlotte was now a married woman and had moved away. Those walks still remained Elizabeth's gold standard for judging amusing pastimes.

Mr. Caversham had so many diverting anecdotes and wry observations that he had proved himself a most agreeable person to spend time with. When Elizabeth rushed to help Miss Bingley, he kept up a good-natured chat with the others, and his light tone served to alleviate any stress brought about by Miss Bingley's predicament. Even the notoriously difficult-to-please

Miss Bingley herself laughed alongside the others.

"Oh dear," Jane said, seeing Miss Bingley sitting down once more with her leg elevated. "It seems Miss Bingley has not recovered at all. She is sure she cannot put weight on the ankle."

Elizabeth shook her head.

"There is really nothing to worry about," she assured her sister. "Miss Bingley slipped while dancing, that is all. It is not an especially hazardous pursuit. She did not fall far. I remain confident that she is all right."

"Well, all right. I am glad to hear your view," said Jane, with a smile.

Elizabeth noted privately that Miss Bingley's ankle actually seemed to have improved greatly. At one point, she swung her leg off the cushion in order to demonstrate the particular dance step which had caused her injury, and Elizabeth noted that she did in fact put weight on it without wincing. There was no doubt in Elizabeth's mind that Miss Bingley had contrived the situation, for reasons known only to herself.

Mrs. Hurst made no attempt to nurse her sister either, adding more ammunition to Elizabeth's theory that it was not a real injury. Even

Mary, the least observant person at Longbourn, seem to have guessed that Miss Bingley's ankle was far less painful than she was making out. Mary would have held forth with a dry lecture on avoiding trips and falls if she had believed Miss Bingley's account.

Really, whatever Miss Bingley had been intending, it could not have worked. Elizabeth gave up wondering what the purpose of the deception was, and returned her thoughts to the ball.

"Have you been dancing, Lizzy?"

"Oh, yes. I managed to break free from Mr. Darcy, and I have been taking a turn with Mr. Caversham this last set."

Jane appraised Mr. Caversham discreetly.

"Ah. And, on a totally unrelated note, have you spotted any gentlemen you would wish to get to know better?"

Elizabeth attempted a mysterious look, then burst into laughter. "I'm afraid not. And I know those two questions were not unrelated, whatever you might claim. But Mr. Caversham is very pleasant indeed. I enjoyed our dance immensely. He has a way of putting his partner at ease, and he has the very best stories to tell."

Jane's eyes twinkled. "Hmm. Perhaps I was right that you may find your husband at the ball tonight."

The sisters chuckled together.

"Mr. Caversham? I think not," Elizabeth said, when the laughter had subsided. "He may have all the attributes one would require in a husband, but I do not get the impression he is looking for a bride in Hertfordshire."

"You never know. And what of Mr. Darcy? Have you changed your mind about him?"

Elizabeth exhaled indignantly. "Changed my mind? No. Mr. Darcy is an adept dancer, but his social skills leave much to be desired. Look how he grimaces at poor Mr. Caversham. No doubt Mr. Caversham is engaging him in an enjoyable discussion, and Mr. Darcy is responding most ungraciously."

Jane looked disconsolate. "So there is no chance of you and Mr. Darcy getting married, I suppose. That is a shame. Perhaps we should consider Mr. Caversham as the prime candidate, in that case."

"Married to *Mr. Darcy?*"

Elizabeth could not stop a loud burst of

laughter from escaping her. Several people turned to look. She dropped her voice again.

"Marry Mr. Darcy? Impossible. A man like Mr. Darcy will never marry. Is there a woman in the whole of England who could thaw his frozen heart?"

"You are too harsh, Lizzy. Mr. Bingley speaks so highly of Mr. Darcy. I cannot believe for a moment that he is not just as warm, caring and loyal as my husband."

"Not all men are like your husband, Jane, regrettable though that is." Elizabeth kissed her sister's cheek. "Not even his closest friends. You are a lucky woman. Enjoy it."

"I am. I do." Jane glowed with pleasure whenever she spoke of her marriage. Elizabeth still found it adorable.

"And are you..." Elizabeth glanced down at Jane's abdomen, and back to her face. "How are you feeling?"

"Quite well. Yes. Quite well, thank you. I find myself a little more tired than usual, but I cannot complain. Mr. Bingley takes every possible step to lighten my burden. Of course, I now have my sisters-in-law on the premises too."

Elizabeth chuckled. "I am sure they create

more work than they help with. But I am very glad to hear you are well, my dear Jane."

They could not continue the conversation, for at that moment, Kitty galloped over to them with a wild look.

"Jane! Lizzy! It is awful. Awful!"

Elizabeth gripped her younger sister's shoulders, to stop her bouncing. "Slow down a moment, Kitty. What are you talking about? What is it? What's awful?"

Kitty was panting so hard, she seemed to find it difficult to speak. At last, she recovered enough to explain herself.

"It's Lydia. We have to help her!"

The orchestra began to play a new tune at that moment, which was upbeat and lively. Kitty only became more agitated.

"Shall we take her somewhere quieter to discuss this?" Jane wondered aloud.

"No time. This is serious." Kitty tugged at Jane's sleeve, and patted Elizabeth's hand on her own shoulder. "Listen. Lydia has been taken. She was at her friend's aunt's house in Portsmouth, and her friend and her aunt went somewhere on an errand while Lydia remained behind, and then they came back, and Lydia had gone. She can't have run off, because she would have left a note for her friend. She's been taken! Someone has taken her!"

Jane and Elizabeth looked at one another in disbelief.

"Taken?" Elizabeth said, trying to work out what Kitty meant. "By whom?"

"We don't know. But her friend thinks it's a sailor. He had been prowling around Lydia the previous night, and had not wanted to take no for an answer. Lydia could be in the middle of the ocean by now, and there's nothing we can do about it."

Kitty began to sob. Jane pulled her close in a comforting embrace.

"How do you know all this, Kitty?" Jane asked.

"Colonel Grayson, my partner for the night. His daughter knows Lydia's friend, the draper's daughter. His daughter received a letter from Lydia's friend this morning and told her father this evening, at this very ball. He immediately relayed it to me, knowing we were related to Lydia."

"This really is awful," Elizabeth muttered. "We need to go to Portsmouth, to find Kitty." She looked around the room, lost in thought. "Shall we tell Mother? She will only worry if she hears the news from someone else. On the other hand, we cannot risk her shrieking the bad news all over the house and condemning Lydia before we have even had a chance to rectify the situation." She shook her head, resolute. "No, we had better not tell Mother."

At this moment, Mr. Darcy left Mr. Caversham's side and approached the sisters. He bowed. "Mrs. Bingley. I could not help noticing your sister's distress. Is there anything with which you need assistance?"

Mr. Caversham followed him over to where the Bennets stood. Mr. Darcy did not seem glad of his continued company.

Jane sighed heavily. "We have a small family problem, Mr. Darcy. We apologise for bringing our discussions to a social event, which is of course inappropriate. Thank you for your kind words of concern."

"Good heavens," Mr. Caversham said. He lingered alongside them all, seemingly ignoring Mr. Darcy's look of disdain. "Is there anything I can do to help?"

Elizabeth smiled gratefully at him. "That's

very kind, but we're just trying to think it over. We would prefer to keep the matter private, for the time being."

"Understood." Mr. Caversham looked startled when Mary took his arm, and, Elizabeth thought, perhaps a little disappointed. He allowed himself to be steered away, but looked meaningfully at Elizabeth.

Before they left the room altogether, he spoke loudly and clearly to Elizabeth. "If you need anything at all, I am yours. Just say the word."

From her position on the two chairs, Miss Bingley looked thrilled at this gossip-worthy turn of phrase. She turned to whisper with Mrs. Hurst.

Elizabeth thanked Mr. Caversham with a brief smile and curtsey, then turned back to Jane.

"I don't know what to do," Jane said, looking agitated.

"You can do nothing. You have a ball to host, and Mr. Bingley would never allow you to cross the counties in your condition."

"What is this talk of crossing counties?" Mr. Darcy would not let the point pass.

Elizabeth sighed impatiently. "Our sister is in Portsmouth. She may be in… difficulty."

Mr. Darcy nodded, and did not press further.

Kitty wrung her hands. "Then what shall we do, Lizzy?"

"We must formulate a plan, and I shall arrange to go to Portsmouth myself."

Jane took Elizabeth's hand. "A lady cannot travel alone like this. Let me send Charles with you."

"Charles needs to be with you. Your need is greater. I shall take my maid, and we shall do our best to find Lydia."

"But what if you cannot find her?"

Elizabeth caught Mr. Darcy's eye. He inclined his head gently by way of acknowledgment, then looked away.

"Let us not think of failure, Jane. I intend to find Lydia. Just leave it with me, and I will decide on the best way to proceed."

Jane embraced Elizabeth. "I shall speak to Mr. Bingley about this."

Elizabeth nodded. "Very well. But I am afraid my mind is made up. I will find Lydia, as soon as possible. I will leave for Portsmouth tonight."

CHAPTER 21

I n conversation with Darcy, Mr. Caversham was as a slippery as an eel. Darcy disliked him from the first moment, purely by instinct.

For some reason, Mr. Caversham had been holding forth on the subject of ladies.

"I was engaged once, long ago. Thank goodness that union never came to pass. She was compromised, and released me from the bond." Mr. Caversham shuddered. "But I did not mind at all. It suits me far better to enjoy the company of multiple ladies, rather than pin myself down to one."

"Is that so?" Darcy said, through clenched teeth.

"Of course, one does not need to tell the ladies everything one is thinking either," he said, with a revolting smirk on his face. "Indeed, I find it most beneficial to keep most of my thoughts to myself."

"I imagine you do," Darcy said. "If one's thoughts are sufficiently unpleasant to risk upsetting people by their expression, I can see how one might prefer to keep them private."

Mr. Caversham laughed emphatically, which only made Darcy dislike him more. "You are a funny man, Mr. Darcy. A very funny man indeed." His laughter tailed off, and his gaze was drawn across the room to the Bennet sisters. "And what of Miss Bennet?"

Darcy gave Mr. Caversham a cold stare. "'*What of Miss Bennet?*' In what sense?"

"Oh, come on, my good man," Mr. Caversham said, with a conspiratorial wink. "We're both gentlemen. I think we both know what we're talking about. Miss Bennet has a lively manner, and a most intriguing way of sizing one up. And she is the eldest unmarried sister, so..." He cleared his throat. "She is perhaps less concerned about propriety than a younger girl may be. Do you know if my path might be clear to—" He looked both ways, to see if anyone was listening. "To getting to know her a little better?"

Mr. Darcy's fists clenched by his side. "I have not the faintest idea what you mean." He had to count to ten to avoid forcibly removing Mr. Caversham from his presence. "If you will excuse me, I must return to my partner."

Mr. Caversham paused mid-word, and it was clear he had not finished talking. But he bowed anyway, and offered a wide smile that reminded Darcy of a wolf.

When Darcy reached them, Miss Bennet was deep in an impassioned conversation with Mrs. Bingley. He bowed to both ladies.

After a few moments of interaction, Jane curtseyed.

"Forgive me, Mr. Darcy. And you, Lizzy. I must attend to my duties, but I shall look out for you again, Lizzy. Please let me know how you wish to proceed. I am in no doubt at all that Mr. Bingley will be only too happy to help in any way we ask."

"I am sure you are right, dear Jane."

Miss Bennet's face was pale, and Darcy felt the urge to step in and fix whatever the problem was. He had not yet got to the bottom of the matter. But it was not his place to enquire. Not, at least, until he were asked.

"Would you like to sit for a while, Miss Bennet?" he said, at last.

"No, thank you. I need to… do something." Miss Bennet's eyes darted this way and that, as though she were preparing to take action of some kind, but did not yet know what.

Darcy nodded again, and adjusted his collar. Miss Bennet was clearly undergoing some sort of emotional difficulty. This was not really his area of expertise. He was used to seeing emotional turmoil in his sister's face, and he had no qualms about dealing with Georgiana's feelings. He had certainly soothed enough of them over the last summer, and been glad to do so.

Yet somehow Miss Bennet was unknown territory. He did not know quite what to say, or how to say it. It was an unfamiliar feeling.

"Would you care for a glass of something restorative?" he said, finally.

She looked almost through him, as though not understanding. Then her expression returned to normal.

"No, thank you Mr. Darcy. I am afraid my mind is elsewhere. It is possible that I will need to leave the ball early, and I pray you excuse me if it proves necessary."

This thought was more deeply disappointing than it ought to have been. Darcy kept that to himself.

"Of course. Then would you allow me to assist you in any way you see fit? I gather the family problem relates to a matter of some delicacy? I must assure you that any help I am able to give will be done so freely, and with the utmost discretion."

She looked at him again, more softly. He noted tears forming in the corners of her deep chestnut eyes. An urge to take her in his arms and comfort her almost overwhelmed him. He forced himself to look over her head to the dancing couples, while he steadied his protective instincts.

"You are kind, Mr. Darcy." Miss Bennet said this in a way that suggested she did not entirely believe he *was* kind. "But it is a family matter, and... we have agreed to keep the details to ourselves."

"I see." Mr. Darcy nodded. "I should not wish to intrude upon private matters."

"No, indeed."

"In that case, I shall cease my enquiries immediately, and trust that you will notify me if there is anything I might do to help."

"Thank you."

Miss Bennet continued wringing her gloved hands, and scanning the room.

"Would you like me to fetch your sisters and mother?"

"Oh! No, not Mamma." Miss Bennet looked quite horrified at the suggestion. "But... Actually, yes. Would you mind asking Kitty and Mary to return to me? And perhaps let Jane know we are in discussion, if you see her? It would be helpful to speak with them."

"Consider it done," Darcy said, with a bow. He headed off on his mission to reunite the Bennet sisters, determined not to pry. How he wished he could do more.

THE REST of the guests were engaged in a rousing game of charades. Hearty laughter boomed out of the ballroom, as Darcy paced by the windows in the adjoining room.

The Bennet sisters, other than Miss Lydia Bennet, were huddled together in deep conversation. Darcy had deliberately placed himself far enough away that he could not hear their chatter, but could still be easily called upon if they required any help.

Bingley emerged from the ballroom, looking concerned. "The snow is heavier. The steward says we should consider ourselves snowed in. It appears that our guests will be forced to stay at Netherfield at least until Saturday afternoon."

Darcy lifted the heavy brocade curtain and peered out. Bingley was right. A thick carpet of snow lay across the ground, and topped every hedge with a white layer. Drifts were already stacking up against the trees, and Darcy imagined that opening an external door would result in a heap of snow on one's boots.

"It will melt by midday tomorrow," he said. "It is a clear night tonight, and that is why it is so cold. But the snow cannot last. We have had a reasonably mild winter thus far."

"I hope you are right, Darcy. Otherwise we will have hundreds of overnight guests, for who knows how long?"

Bingley locked hands behind his back and watched the Bennet ladies, with their animated interchanges. He said nothing to Darcy. Darcy felt obliged to remark on it.

"Bingley, I am staying out of the private matter under discussion, but if there is anything I can do—"

"Say no more. I know you are always willing to help. Thank you, Darcy."

Bingley was clearly not going to elaborate. Despite his protestations of discretion, Darcy could not help wondering why the secrecy was needed. A family member had an awkward problem to deal with, but what could be so serious?

Immediately, he rebuked himself. It was none of his concern, and he had his own family issues anyway. Georgiana was his priority. Nobody else was. If Miss Bennet wished him to intervene in any way, she would inform him. Until then, he would be sure to converse on other topics, that were not controversial, and which would take her mind off her family concerns. That would be best.

Resolute, he paced the room. But he could never quite take his eyes off Miss Bennet. That, he could not talk himself out of.

Miss Bingley, and Mr. and Mrs. Hurst, came stumbling out of the ballroom, laughing uproariously. All three of them had indulged in many glasses of liquor, judging by their unsteady gait and their glazed expressions.

"Oh come, Darcy!" shrieked Miss Bingley. "Come and dance, I insist. We're all abandoning the partners we were stuck with. It's a silly game. Silly, silly, silly. Let us go back to the dance floor and show these bumpkins how it is done."

Darcy stared at her in disbelief.

Bingley took her elbow. "It is time to stop drinking for the evening, Caroline."

"*Stop* drinking? How else am I to enjoy this hateful ball?" Miss Bingley laughed, as though this was the funniest thing she had ever heard. "*Au contraire*, my dear brother. I shall require far more to drink."

She spotted the Bennets, sitting in a corner together, and pointed a wavering finger at them.

"Oh look, it's the Bennet girls. So fine and accomplished a party you never did see!" She staggered, then corrected her balance. "Miss Bennet! You do not object if I steal away your partner, I hope? I wish to dance with him again. Nobody else will do."

Miss Bennet looked up, blankly. Then she shook her head. "I do not object in the least, Miss Bingley. As you wish." She returned her attention to her sisters.

"I do not consent to being 'stolen'," Darcy said calmly. "Please control yourself, Miss Bingley. Do not show up your brother while he is hosting his first ball. You are better than this."

"Not as good as the perfect Eliza Bennet though, of course," slurred Miss Bingley. "Oh, I see how you look at the dumpy country girl. Don't think I haven't noticed!"

"Caroline!" Bingley rebuked her. "I will thank you to keep a civil tongue in your head. And please be quiet." He beckoned to a passing footman. "Would you retrieve Miss Bingley's maid for me please? Somebody needs to take her up to bed."

"Oh, I can think of one or two candidates," Miss Bingley said, raising a single eyebrow at Darcy. He turned away at once, appalled.

"That is enough!" Bingley snapped. His tone was so rarely sharp, it seemed to shock Miss Bingley into silence. She cast a sullen look around the room, and stormed off. Mrs. Hurst and Mr. Hurst trailed after her, looking tired and bewildered.

"My apologies, Darcy." Bingley looked mortified. "I have never seen Caroline in such disarray. Heaven only knows what she thinks she is doing."

Darcy clapped him on the back. "No need to say a word. Apparently feelings are running high all around."

"Yes, and we now will all be stuck in one house together until the snow clears. Dear oh dear."

A movement in the corner of Darcy's eye drew his attention back to the sisters. Miss Bennet had stood up and was making her way out of the group.

"Mr. Bingley," she said, approaching him with a determined look on her face. "I must leave Netherfield at once. I need to reach Portsmouth as soon as possible."

CHAPTER 22

The Bennet sisters had reached an uneasy decision. Somehow, they must retrieve Lydia from Portsmouth. Moreover, they must do so without letting the details of Lydia's behaviour reach the wider public.

They did not wish to bother their mother with the troubling news about Lydia, particularly given Mrs. Bennet's tendency to take to her bed at the slightest provocation. Even more importantly, they did not want to worry their father while he was still recovering from a serious illness.

But something certainly needed to be done. Lydia could still be somewhere in Portsmouth, with the scoundrel who had taken her. If they left it much longer, she could be taken overseas.

Lydia's reputation was already in dangerous waters, but what if her life were at stake too?

"There is only one solution left open to us," Elizabeth announced. "Somehow, one of us needs to get to Portsmouth, and do her utmost to find Lydia."

It was obvious to them all that Elizabeth was volunteering herself for the job. As none of the others wished to take on such a fiendishly difficult duty, they were only too happy for Elizabeth to offer herself.

She stood and informed Mr. Bingley that she was leaving. When he told her it was impossible, she could hardly take in the refusal.

"The snow is falling heavily, Miss Bennet. It is terribly treacherous to even attempt to travel in these conditions. I beg that you wait until the snow melts."

"But the turning of the weather could take days," Elizabeth cried. "Possibly even weeks. We cannot wait."

"We have not had especially cold temperatures these past few weeks," Mr. Darcy interjected. "The snow will not settle for long. The clear skies will make way for cloud, and we shall have warmer January days. This snowfall will have cleared within a day."

"You cannot be sure of that."

Mr. Darcy never seemed to accept a difference of opinion, and now was no exception. "On the contrary I am confident that—"

Elizabeth interrupted him, in her desperation. "Please, Mr. Darcy. There is no time to debate the matter. I really must get to Portsmouth." She looked around wildly, as though something in the room would suggest to her the perfect solution. "Mr. Bingley, may I borrow a carriage? I really cannot take ours, as Mother will be stranded here, and also because it will mean I would need to furnish her with an explanation. We prefer not to worry her, as yet."

Mr. Bingley looked at his wife with love and concern. "Mrs. Bingley, please. I must insist that your sister postpones this plan. I am quite serious about the snow. Leaving Netherfield tonight is not possible. And that is quite aside from the fact that a lady should not travel so far alone, or with a single servant. It is unthinkable."

Jane looked at Elizabeth, and back to her husband. She seemed torn in two by the conflicting viewpoints.

Mr. Darcy stepped forward once more. "Miss Bennet, could somebody else take a message to Portsmouth for you? If we send a couple of the hardiest footmen, they may manage to reach the main roads before they become impassable. Their journey must necessarily be due south, at any rate, and so they may find the weather naturally improves as they progress."

Elizabeth bit her lip. She did not want to share her family's intimate secrets with a pair of servants. Footmen were renowned for their love of gossip, and of the attention they received downstairs when they shared revealing anecdotes.

On the other hand, she did need somebody to reach Portsmouth, as soon as possible.

"If I may accompany them, then certainly."

Mr. Bingley shook his head. "Oh no. It would not be advisable to travel yourself, Miss Bennet. And might I remind you that you are a lady? You cannot travel with two footmen, regardless of the circumstances."

"I will take a chaperone. My ladies' maid is a married woman."

"Your father would not hear of it. In his stead, I cannot approve it either."

"One of us needs to be there," Elizabeth insisted, with a steely firmness to her voice.

Mr. Darcy and Mr. Bingley exchanged glances.

"In that case, Miss Bennet," Mr. Darcy said, "*I* shall accompany you, and we shall find ourselves a chaperone somewhere. Bingley, please call my sister. I will need to inform her of my whereabouts. Will you look after her for the few days that I am gone?"

"But of course, Darcy."

Miss Bennet stared at him. "That will not be necessary, Mr. Darcy. Please, remain here at Netherfield with Miss Darcy. She needs you, and that is more important to you than our family business."

"I cannot agree to let you go alone, Miss Bennet."

"I shall not be alone. We have just established that a pair of sturdy servants will be accompanying me, and a chaperone."

Mr. Bingley shook his head, frowning in confusion. "Miss Bennet, we have just established that this is *not* possible."

Mr. Darcy looked quite taken aback, as though the idea of Elizabeth's refusing his offer had never crossed his mind. His over-confidence annoyed her. The man was always so presumptuous, and so sure he was right about everything.

He seemed to accept her final answer, however, and backed away. Taking up a position on the far side of the room, he stood proudly with his hands behind his back.

"Should we perhaps consider Mr. Darcy's offer?" Mary was at Elizabeth's shoulder, talking with her hand over her mouth. It was a pantomime of discretion. "We need to find Lydia before she is taken anywhere else. That is our priority. Mr. Bingley will not allow you to leave with just servants, but he may concede the point if Mr. Darcy promises to look after you, and if a respectable chaperone may be found. Although Mr. Darcy may not be your first choice of travelling companion, would he not be useful in this regard?"

Elizabeth glanced back at Mr. Darcy. He caught her watching him, and nodded respectfully at her. She looked back at Mary.

"I do not wish to involve strangers in our private business. If word gets out about Lydia, we are all ruined. There must be another way."

"Wait here." Kitty leaped from her seat and

scampered for the door. Elizabeth, Mary and Jane looked at one another.

"Any idea what that girl is doing now?" Mary asked.

Elizabeth shrugged "None whatsoever."

They soon realised, however, when Kitty returned arm-in-arm with Mr. Caversham.

Out of the corner of her eye, Elizabeth noticed Mr. Darcy take a step forward, giving Mr. Caversham a dark look.

"What are you doing, Kitty?" Elizabeth asked, with a warning look in her eye.

Kitty was oblivious. "Mr. Caversham says he will help us. He is willing to take one of us to Portsmouth in a carriage, and he says he will overlook the necessity of a chaperone. If we do not tell anyone of the breach of protocol, neither will he."

"Perhaps it should be you who accompanies me, Miss Bennet," Mr. Caversham said, smiling broadly at Elizabeth. "No need to trouble anyone else then."

Elizabeth frowned at her silly sister Kitty. "You have spoken to others about our... concern?"

Mr. Caversham raised his hands, in an

expression of innocence. "Oh, please. You have nothing to fear. I am the very soul of discretion."

"I did not give him any details," Kitty added.

"Then why has he offered to help?" Mary asked. Elizabeth wondered the same thing.

"Let's just say I have a soft spot for damsels in distress." He grinned, his face lit up with the same sunshine glow of positivity that had turned Elizabeth's head earlier in the evening.

"We are not *damsels*," Elizabeth said, but her voice had softened a little. Mr. Caversham had nothing to gain by offering his help. He was evidently a selfless kind of man who liked to feel useful. There was nothing wrong with that. She still did not intend to talk to him about the fact that her sister's reputation was close to destruction, or share any of the other shameful details. But she was grateful for his offer. He meant well, she was sure.

Mr. Caversham stepped back with a deep bow, to allow the sisters to discuss the matter further. He stood a few feet away from Mr. Darcy, with a benevolent look on his face.

Elizabeth noted that Mr. Darcy was glowering at Mr. Caversham, but ignored it. Mr.

Darcy was frequently ill-tempered, and there was no point trying to fathom his reasons.

"My main concern is finding Lydia before she is transported elsewhere," she said to her sisters. "By any means necessary."

Mary sighed. "I'm most worried about Mamma's reaction. She will be bedridden for weeks if she discovers Lydia is missing with a man. Our reputations will be ruined, and Mamma will never recover. She is pinning everything on our family's good name. Look how thrilled she was when Jane married Mr. Bingley. She wants us all to find a good match like Jane."

"No chance of that if the news about Lydia gets out," grumbled Kitty. "Who is going to believe that she is forcibly detained? People will believe she was a willing participant in a scandal. Then our chances of marrying well will be less than nought."

"Let us not dwell on our own marriage prospects at this time," Elizabeth said, sternly. "I shall go to Portsmouth with two footmen, my married maid, and perhaps Mr. Caversham, if he may be spared."

"Will you take Mr. Darcy with you too?" said Kitty, twirling a curl around her finger. "If not... well, I should not object if you want to leave him behind. I can look after him for you if you wish."

"I think I can guess why you're saying that," murmured Mary, rolling her eyes heavenward. "Mr. Darcy is handsome, Kitty, but there is no need to swoon over him so."

"I am not swooning!"

"Girls, please." Jane held up an open hand before them, in a gesture of calm. "I do not wish you to go anywhere, Lizzy, least of all if it breaches social rules, but I agree we need to take some sort of action. But my husband is right about the snow. Nobody can drive a carriage in these conditions."

Elizabeth exclaimed in frustration. "This is too much. We do not have a moment to lose."

"I know, Lizzy. I know. We will pray that the snow disappears quickly."

It was not what Elizabeth wanted to hear, but she had no choice in the matter for now. Pacing the floor impatiently, she prayed silently that the snow would clear.

From the ballroom, raucous laughter drifting out. She was sure she could detect her mother's shrill chortle over all the others. At least Mamma could enjoy the ball. Elizabeth would make sure her mother's evening was not ruined, the way her own evening had been. The secret of Lydia's predicament would remain with the sisters.

CHAPTER 23

The feast was sumptuous, but Elizabeth was not in the mood to enjoy it. While others were spooning soup and laughing together, she found herself staring at the wall. It was difficult to relax when all she could think about was finding Lydia before she was lost for good.

"The soup is very good," ventured a soft voice on her right.

Elizabeth turned to see Miss Carrington smiling shyly at her from the adjacent chair. She must have returned from wherever she had been hiding. Elizabeth had not even noticed Miss Carrington taking the chair beside her.

"My apologies, Miss Carrington. I was miles away."

"You really should taste it. I do not think I have tasted soup this flavoursome in a long while."

Elizabeth picked up her spoon and obliged. Miss Carrington was right. It was wasted on her in this state, however.

"Are you enjoying the ball, Miss Carrington?"

Miss Carrington smiled and looked down at her bowl. "It is most diverting. I confess I am not much inclined towards large social events, but this ball is certainly agreeable."

"Do you prefer to spend time alone, then, or with small groups of others?"

"What I prefer most of all is to read." Miss Carrington blushed, as though she had revealed a most intimate truth about herself. "I am never happier than when I am left to my own devices in my father's library. But when I am in company, I suppose I prefer small groups."

"I cannot help but wonder why you agreed to accompany Miss Bingley to Netherfield." Elizabeth smiled kindly at her. "Did you have no family events to attend?"

"Miss Bingley has been very kind, but..." Miss Carrington faltered. "She advised me to mix with others as soon as possible after my... difficult episode. And she was quite insistent about it."

Miss Carrington's cheeks burned red now, and Elizabeth resolved not to ask any questions about the 'difficult episode'. Presumably, Miss Carrington was referring to her broken engagement. She wondered what kind of misdeed the fellow could have done to warrant Miss Carrington breaking off their union.

But she did not need to enquire. Miss Carrington volunteered the information.

"I was quite broken-hearted some weeks ago, and Miss Bingley felt it would be best if I came with her to see her brother. She has taken me under her wing, you see."

Elizabeth felt there had to be an ulterior motive in there somewhere, but she just smiled. "That's nice. I am sorry to hear of your broken heart."

"The man I was to marry decided he would do better elsewhere."

Elizabeth put down her spoon in amazement. "Your fiancé called off the engagement himself? That is highly irregular." And most ungentlemanly, she omitted to say.

"Well, no. He managed to persuade me to do it. But he told me over and over again how he would hate to wake up in the same house as me every day, and how he would take a mistress the day after the wedding, and so many other things to paint the picture of a miserable marriage. In the end, I did as I knew he wanted me to do. I ended our engagement, and freed him. It was unavoidable, if I wished to have any peace of mind again."

"How on earth did you become engaged to such an unpleasant man in the first place?" The question slipped out before Elizabeth had a chance to temper the heat of it. She regretted its directness once she had said it, but it was a little late.

"Our parents pushed us together. Our mothers had grown up as close confidantes and it had been assumed since my birth that we would marry. It suited everybody."

"Everybody except the two of you."

"Well, I…" She dabbed at her mouth with her napkin. "I had grown rather attached to him, I confess."

Miss Carrington now had tears in her eyes. Elizabeth felt terribly sorry for her. So she had not wanted to lose the ungrateful wretch, but had done so because it was what he wanted. And now she was paying the price of a reduced trustworthiness. It was all so horribly unfair.

"It sounds as though you may have had a lucky escape, Miss Carrington. Better to remain a spinster for life than to tie yourself to a husband who does not warrant the name of *gentleman*."

Miss Carrington tried to smile, but did not quite manage it.

"I know you are right, Miss Bennet. You are very kind."

Elizabeth patted her new friend's arm. "Would you prefer to be alone to recover your composure?"

"I feel I would recover better if I had some space to think about something else. But for now, I have to be at Netherfield. If I am here, I am very grateful for the company of kind people." She smiled at Elizabeth. "Miss Darcy has become a friend, and I wish she was out already so that she could enjoy this ball too."

"Yes, Miss Darcy is probably tossing and turning in her bed-chamber, wishing she was downstairs with the merriment." Elizabeth remembered how excited she had been to make her début. "I am sure she will be very happy to be reunited with you tomorrow."

One of the heavy curtains at the back of the room had been moved aside, as some guests pushed joyfully past it. Elizabeth craned her neck to see if she could spot snowflakes against the night sky. She could not get a good enough view.

"Will you excuse me for a moment, Miss Carrington? I need to check the weather."

"Of course."

Elizabeth hurried to the tall windows and looked out. The snowfall had stopped. Unfortunately, the snow on the ground was thicker than ever. A thick white coating covered everything, and made the grounds brighter than they should be at that time of night. The moon was fully visible in a cloudless sky, and the blue tint of moonlight shimmered across the snow. Elizabeth found the stark winter landscape beautiful, but it was also most disheartening.

"Have you made any further plans, Miss Bennet? Is there anything you need?"

Mr. Darcy was behind her. She turned to face him.

"There is nothing more to be done, Mr.

Darcy. Evidently, the snow is too deep to travel by carriage. Unless I am to walk to Portsmouth, my plan has been scuppered."

She felt guilty for snapping at him. It was not Mr. Darcy's fault that it had snowed. She should not take out her frustration on him.

On the other hand, he *was* responsible for some of the maelstrom of unfamiliar emotions swirling in her heart. She was still a little perturbed about that.

The thought of Lydia's good name being ruined forever upset her deeply. She was a silly young girl, prone to lapses of judgment, and she certainly should not have remained at Weymouth with her friend without seeking the approval of her family. But she did not deserve her fate. If Elizabeth could save her from complete ruination, she would move heaven and earth to do so.

But what if it were too late? What if news of Lydia's predicament reached the wider public? Lizzy might be able to save her from abduction, but what if she were too late to rescue her good name?

What if the entire family was affected by it? She knew her prospects of ever marrying would be nil. Kitty had been right about that, at least.

"Mr. Darcy," she said, suddenly. "Do you think a person can ever recover from a damaged reputation?"

CHAPTER 24

Darcy thought immediately of the unctuous Mr. Caversham. He had shown himself to be a vile specimen, treating women as playthings and disregarding their virtue. Darcy felt pure contempt for Mr. Caversham's smooth patter.

Had Mr. Caversham managed to wheedle his way into Miss Bennet's esteem? The thought revulsed him. He suppressed the response he wanted to give, which was harsh and scathing, and answered her calmly.

"No, Miss Bennet. I think a bad reputation is usually well-earned."

"So you do not think it possible for society's faith in a person to be restored, once lost?"

"Society rarely withdraws its approval for no

reason. If a person has earned himself a social reprimand, it is unlikely to be unjustly bestowed."

"Is that so?" Miss Bennet seemed upset by his remarks, which confused him.

He hated the idea that Miss Bennet was trying to rehabilitate Mr. Caversham in her own eyes. That rascal was not fit to clean the lady's boots.

"Of course. Miss Bennet, those who flout society's rules are not clever, or glamorous, in any way. They are shameful, and their isolation is self-imposed. We do not need to pity them. They chose their own actions freely, and should be judged accordingly."

"And if they did not choose freely?" Miss Bennet appeared to be fighting strong emotions. "If they were drawn into a situation far beyond that which they ever envisaged?"

Were they still talking about Mr. Caversham? Darcy supposed they must be. It seemed Miss Bennet was rather more attached to him than Darcy had thought. A boulder seemed to settle in his stomach.

"Every man is bound by his decisions. There can be no exceptions."

With a sob, Miss Darcy turned on her heel and fled.

Mr. Darcy's mouth fell open. He had no idea what had just caused Miss Bennet to leave so suddenly.

Should he go after her?

Would that only make matters worse?

A gnawing sense of guilt forced him to pursue her, at a distance. He watched as Elizabeth fell into the arms of her older sister, who embraced her with something of the same turmoil on her face.

He could not proceed further. It was not his place to intrude on sisterly affection. He was just glad that Miss Bennet had found a source of comfort so quickly.

If he could have worked out why she had become so upset, he would make sure he never did it again. But he could not. It was quite unfathomable.

Feeling somewhat self-conscious, Darcy removed himself to the side of the room, and watched to ensure Miss Bennet was quite all right. There was little else he could do at that moment.

❄

"Mrs. Bingley?"

Miss Bennet lifted her head from her sister's shoulder. Mrs. Bingley turned to the footman, who approached her now in a state of great dishevelment.

"Richard?" Miss Bennet said, wide-eyed. "Have you just come all the way from Longbourn?"

"Yes, ma'am. The snow is too thick for a carriage, so I walked. I am afraid it took me a lot longer than I had anticipated." He shook the snow from his breeches, and shivered.

Mrs. Bingley called over one of her own footmen. "Please fetch a warm blanket and some brandy. One of my family's footmen has just arrived on foot and is very cold."

"Do you bring news from Longbourn?" Miss Bennet asked him. Her face had grown exceedingly pale.

"I am afraid so, ma'am. Mr. Bennet has taken a turn for the worse."

Mrs. Bingley squealed, and her hand flew to her mouth.

Miss Bennet grasped him by both arms.

"Has the doctor called?"

"No, ma'am. The steward sent for him some hours previously, but he has not managed to travel in the snow. We hope he may come by mid-morning tomorrow."

"That may be too late." Miss Bennet took her sister's face in her own hands. "Jane, there is no time to discuss it. Run and fetch Mamma. She must be told. We need to get back to Longbourn as quickly as possible. I will find Mary and Kitty."

The sisters rushed off in opposite directions. Darcy saw the footman shiver, though he was now wrapped in a thick blanket and clutched a glass of brandy. Darcy took him a chair and guided him gently into it.

"Thank you sir," said Richard, through chattering teeth. "Much obliged to you."

Darcy mused on what he had just heard. Mr. Bennet's health was in peril. This crisis on top of the earlier crisis would prove insurmountable for the sisters, if they did not accept any help. He was determined to offer his, and ensure they did not refuse it this time.

"You must warm up as soon as possible, Richard. Stay here while you recover."

"Yes, sir. Thanking you again, sir."

Darcy left the warmly-wrapped Richard to his brandy, and hurried to find the Bennets.

HE COULD NOT FIND the sisters indoors. By chance, some guests had pulled back a heavy curtain in the ballroom, to view the snow, and Darcy spotted movement out of a rear window.

Miss Bennet and Mrs. Bingley were conducting a heated discussion outside, in knee-deep snow.

He rushed out to join them.

"But we cannot be in two places at once, Lizzy. Be reasonable." Mrs. Bingley's voice was desperate.

Miss Bennet held up a hand to her sister. "This is no time for reason, Jane. Our father may be dying. And our sister may be lost to us forever. Can you see any element of reason in either of those two events?"

Darcy spotted Mrs. Bennet, standing in the doorway. He approached her, and bowed.

"Please sit down, Mrs. Bennet. You have had a shock."

"Oh, you are very kind, Mr. Darcy. Very kind.

I knew you would be kind, from the first moment I heard of you."

Darcy did not know what to make of that, but he overlooked it. Bowing, he turned to the open doorway. The wind chilled the little vestibule, and lines of snow tracked across the threshold from the moment the door had been opened.

Neither Mrs. Bingley nor Miss Bennet wore any outdoor layers at all. They were outside in freezing temperatures, wearing only formal evening gowns.

"Mrs. Bingley," he called. "Miss Bennet. Please come back inside. You will catch your deaths of cold if you do not."

"I need to leave Netherfield now," Miss Bennet insisted.

She was quite the most stubborn creature he had ever encountered.

"And where will you go, Miss Bennet? To Portsmouth? Or to Longbourn? In which direction do you plan to travel?"

She stared blankly at him, and he noticed her quivering. This was ridiculous. He was not about to stand by while she gave herself frostbite.

He strode into the garden and lifted her up.

Mrs. Bingley gasped, but Miss Bennet made no sound.

"Follow us indoors please Mrs. Bingley," he called, as he transported Miss Bennet into the house. Mrs. Bingley obliged.

Setting Miss Bennet down on the Turkish rug, he closed and locked the door.

"Please do not tell me to leave you to the privacy of your plan. I cannot, and I will not. It seems to me that you have two conflicting predicaments. One requires you to travel three miles home, as urgently as possible. I would venture that this is the most pressing of the two. The other requires you to travel to Portsmouth. Logistically, this is going to prove more difficult. Not insurmountably so, but it is less straightforward. Am I correct?"

Miss Bennet seemed to have given up resisting his offers of help. She nodded.

"Then this is what we shall do. Mrs. Bennet, you shall travel home to Longbourn with your four daughters, the very second the footmen can clear a path to the main road and judge safe passage to be realistic."

The ladies nodded.

"I shall go to Portsmouth with a manservant,

and undertake whatever business it is that you have there."

This made Mrs. Bingley gape at Miss Bennet, but she did not flinch.

"All right," she said at last. "I do not wish to burden you, sir. But I cannot now go to Portsmouth and miss what may be our final hours with our father. I shall relate our problem to you, Mr. Darcy. If you still wish to assist us, we should be grateful to accept your offer. We have no choice in the matter."

Mrs. Bingley nodded gravely.

"Then that is settled," Darcy said. "I shall make the arrangements at once."

Before he could leave, there was an almighty squeal from the front of the room. Everyone turned to look at the source of the commotion.

Mr. Caversham was standing before Miss Carrington, looking thoroughly astonished.

"You!" she wailed, pointing at him. "*You!*"

Mr. Caversham looked around, trying to catch everyone's eye. "I really don't know what—"

"How can you show your face here? *Haven't you done enough?*"

Mr. Bingley intervened. "Miss Carrington, what is it? Whatever is the matter?"

"This man — this cad," she cried. "This is the man I was engaged to. This is the man who insulted me, and made me — yes, *made* me — break off our promises. And Miss Bingley brought me to Netherfield deliberately, knowing he would be here tonight."

She turned to look around the room, a wild-eyed expression on her face. Eventually, she spotted Miss Bingley slumped in a corner, with her sister and brother-in-law.

"How *could* you, Miss Bingley?"

Miss Bingley held her glass aloft and snickered. "Oh, hush. The worm has turned, has it? You really don't need to shout, dear. We can all hear you perfectly."

Mr. Bingley was incensed. "Is this true, Caroline? Did you bring your friend here deliberately to run into Mr. Caversham, for... for sport?"

Miss Bingley grinned malevolently. "Oh, relax. Nothing happened. It was funny to poke the shy little thing to see what she did. Rather like capturing a frog and prodding it to make it hop. Life gets terribly boring in the countryside. I wanted a pastime."

"Leave the room at once," Mr. Bingley said, with quiet menace. "I shall deal with you later."

Darcy checked to see if his friend needed any reinforcements, but he did not. He nodded at Darcy, still looking livid.

Darcy turned back to the Bennets. "Well, the spectacle seems to be over. If you can apprise me of the situation, Miss Bennet, I shall then take my leave of you. I wish you all the very best of luck in returning to Longbourn swiftly."

Miss Bennet stepped forward, and began to tell him all about Miss Lydia.

CHAPTER 25

M r. Darcy had been right. By noon the
following day, the snow was beginning
to melt. Where previously the grounds had been
carpeted with a sparkling white layer, it had
turned to slush, tracked back and forth by birds
and squirrels.

The guests began to filter out of Netherfield,
to return to their homes. Nobody had slept, of
course, but then nobody had really expected to.
They were only a few hours later than they had
anticipated, and nobody seemed in the least
inconvenienced by the later ending to the ball.

Elizabeth, her mother and her sisters climbed
into their carriage as soon as the conditions were
passable. Mr. Bingley made sure theirs was the
first in line. He remained behind, and promised

Mr. Darcy that he would take good care of Miss Darcy in his absence. Miss Carrington assured him that she would entertain Miss Darcy, and Mr. Bingley's kindly Aunt and Uncle Glastonford remained at Netherfield in order to watch over the girl too.

The journey back to Longbourn seemed to take an age. Of course, the road was icy in places, and the driver had to be adept at steering the horses away from the more hazardous patches. Elizabeth knew they were moving as fast as they could, but the anxiety was unavoidable. She could not help fidgeting as she sat, drumming her hands on her lap and twirling a stray curl.

The moment Longbourn appeared in the distance, Elizabeth was half out of her seat.

Her mother pulled her back onto the seat beside her. "Sit back, Lizzy. The road is too bumpy not to stay sitting down. You will fall, and that will be no use to anybody."

By the time the oak door was opened for them, Elizabeth had already leaned out of the carriage window and unfastened the door, before the driver could even get there.

She ran into the hallway and headed for the stairs, without even removing her travelling-cloak. She slipped it off as she climbed the stairs, and dropped it over the bannister, without another thought.

She had to get to her father.

When she reached his bedchamber and opened the door, she could not stifle a gasp. Mr. Bennet looked worse than she had even imagined. Somehow, she could only picture her father reading, or asleep in his bed, propped up with pillows. But now, his face had changed beyond all measure. In just the hours since they left for the ball, it seemed that he had transformed into someone else entirely. His face was sallow, and his eyes were sunken. His breath rattled in his chest.

The doctor stepped forward from the shadows at the edge of the room. Elizabeth had not even noticed him standing there.

"He is not taking any food or drink," the doctor said, solemnly. "He is not asleep, though he may not be able to respond. But he will be glad of your company."

Elizabeth sat gingerly on the edge of the bed and took her father's hand. It was limp and cool to the touch. A tear slid down her face and splashed onto her lap.

Her mother had reached the room now, and she took the other side of the bed, throwing herself to her knees and wailing.

"Oh, Mr. Bennet! How can you have done this, the moment we turned our backs? Could you not have waited until the winter was over? It is just like you to choose the most disagreeable time possible. You always—" She broke off, unable to contain her sobbing, and threw herself upon his chest. "My dear Mr. Bennet. How I have loved you."

Jane stood behind Elizabeth and put her arms around her sister. Mary and Kitty crept in and stood at the foot of the bed, weeping softly.

It was a scene none of them had dreamed they would come home to.

"If you wish to say anything to Mr. Bennet," the doctor murmured, "you would be wise to take the opportunity to do so now."

"How long?" Elizabeth asked at once. "How long does Father have left?"

"It cannot be predicted with certainty. Perhaps a few days. Perhaps a few hours. Best to seize each moment and leave no loose ends. That is my advice."

The doctor bowed, and withdrew from the room.

"Lydia is never going to see Father again," sobbed Kitty. Mary hugged her tightly.

With the heaviest of hearts, and a good deal of tears, the five women surrounded Mr. Bennet with love.

Three days later, when they were all together, it was over.

As was his preference in life, Mr. Bennet slipped away to the heavenly realm with no fuss at all.

He had found peace at last.

CHAPTER 26

Elizabeth's black bombazine dress fell heavily around her ankles. She sat before the looking glass, gazing blankly at her reflection.

Her maid approached her timidly, to adjust her hair. Elizabeth agreed without enthusiasm. It was impossible to muster any eagerness to bury one's beloved father.

Jane came into the room, in her mourning outfit.

"Gracious, Lizzy. You are not ready." She sat on the end of Elizabeth's bed. "We are all sorry to be attending the funeral today. You are not alone, my dear sister."

"I know." Elizabeth fought back the tears which came regularly for the last four days, since her father had passed away. "I was thinking back to the night of the ball. It was only a week ago. I sat here, dressing up and preening for a social event, when I should have remained here with Father. Perhaps he would not have taken a turn for the worse if he had been attended."

Jane took Elizabeth's hand. "You know that is not true, Lizzy. He was not alone. The servants were highly attuned to his needs, and the doctor was sent for just as soon as he felt worse. There was no delay in attending to his requirements. Please do not blame yourself. I promise you, there was nothing you could have done."

Elizabeth took a deep breath and steadied herself. "Very well. I will stop dwelling on the things I cannot change, and be strong for Mamma."

"That is a good idea." Jane kissed her sister's forehead, dodging the maid's curling comb as she did so. "Have you heard any word from Lydia since the ball? Or from Mr. Darcy?"

"No, I have not. It has been a week since he set off too."

"How long is the journey from Hertfordshire to Portsmouth?"

"Very long. It is over one hundred miles. That

means at least two days each way, and Mr. Darcy left on a Friday, which means he must have taken three days. There is no travel possible on a Sunday."

Jane nodded. "Quite so. In that case, Mr. Darcy must have reached Portsmouth by Tuesday. Today is Friday. Unless he found Lydia immediately, he could not be back today. I do hope he manages to send a message to us, however."

Elizabeth agreed. "It is such a shame that Lydia was not here for Father's passing. She will have no idea, and will have a terrible shock when she returns."

There was a knock at the door. Jane went to open it, and found one of the maids standing there, looking bashful.

"Please, Mrs. Bingley, Mr. Collins is downstairs. Says he needs to speak to Mrs. Bennet. But she has given us strict instructions not to disturb her before the, er, carriages arrive." She was reluctant to say the word "funeral", and somehow Elizabeth felt grateful that she sidestepped it. "What would you like me to tell him, ma'am?"

Jane groaned. "Tell him I will receive him in the drawing room."

The maid left to follow her instructions.

"Lizzy, do not worry about this. Mr. Collins has inherited Longbourn, but he cannot turn out the family this quickly. He must wait for Mamma to make other arrangements."

"What other arrangements?"

"Well, we shall bring you all to live with us at Netherfield."

"Mamma will hate that. She has always dreaded not being the mistress of her own home. You know she will give you no end of trouble, every day of the week."

Jane smiled. "I know. We are prepared for that. But honestly, Lizzy, do you think we would see you turned out on the street? Not a bit of it."

Jane leaned over and embraced her sister. The maid stood back, respectfully.

"Thank you, Jane. You are a wonderful sister. I am so glad you are in a position to help like this, and I am so sorry for imposing upon you and your marriage."

"Nonsense! We are all family. Mr. Bingley is as resolute as I."

Elizabeth smiled, through the stray tears which threatened to burst forth again. She only wished Lydia could be here to pay her last respects to their father. It did not seem right to hold the funeral without her. But they could not wait any longer to bury Mr. Bennet. Four days had been quite long enough.

She would be strong for her mother, and for her sisters. She would not waver.

With the pain of grief still fresh in her chest, she set her mind to the important business of grooming. It was better than no distraction at all.

THE CARRIAGES ARRIVED. Mrs. Bennet and four of her daughters assembled in the hallway, dressed in their black mourning gowns. Mrs. Bennet's face bore the signs of deep sorrow, but she held her head high. Elizabeth resolved to do the same.

"We shall not think of Lydia today," Mrs. Bennet announced. "It will make the day even harder. We must trust that she is safe, and that she will return to us in good time."

"What if she is not safe? What if she has been taken, and that is why we have heard no word from her?" Kitty dissolved into tears again, and Elizabeth embraced her.

"It is the hardest thing I have ever asked you

to do," Elizabeth said, "but I need you to be strong today, Kitty. I need you to hold yourself together, for Father's sake. We must pay our last respects to him. He is in a better place now. Let us devote today to his memory, and think of our other worries afterwards."

Kitty nodded, and dabbed at her nose with her handkerchief.

The day was dim and grey. It was cold, as January days usually were, but there was no snow, nor wind. Instead, a dull stillness seemed to have settled over the landscape.

As they left the house to enter the carriage, Mary shouted out "Look!"

Elizabeth rushed to see what her sister meant. In the distance, a carriage rumbled down the Longbourn driveway.

"It is not Lydia," Mrs. Bennet said. "We know it is not possible that it is Lydia. I do not recognise the carriage, for one thing."

But Mrs. Bennet was mistaken.

Before the carriage even came to a halt, they saw Lydia's face at the window. She looked haunted and thinner, but she was alive and well.

They threw themselves upon her before she had even stepped fully out of the carriage.

"Oh, Lydia! Oh, my darling!" Mrs. Bennet wept with joy to be reunited with her youngest daughter. The other sisters were similarly joyful.

"I am so sorry, Mamma," Lydia wept. "So very sorry."

Her face was wan, and her tone genuinely contrite. She had clearly had a great fright.

Elizabeth held her close, her heart full.

It took a few minutes before it registered with Elizabeth that Lydia could not have arrived at Longbourn alone. She opened the carriage door a little further and looked inside.

Mr. Darcy sat in the corner, smiling. Next to him sat a plump middle-aged woman, wiping her eyes.

"Mr. Darcy," whispered Elizabeth. "You did it. You brought our Lydia home."

When he emerged from the carriage, it was all she could do to resist embracing him too.

"I am sorry it took so long," he said.

CHAPTER 27

The funeral had not been an enjoyable event, naturally, but it had been as dignified and loving as Elizabeth had hoped.

Mr. Darcy had returned to Netherfield when they entered the church. His companion, Lydia's friend's aunt, had insisted on travelling home to Weymouth by post-chaise. Mr. Darcy had insisted on paying all her travel and lodging costs in full — "It is the least I can do, madam" — and she had accepted with a hearty grin and a wink at Elizabeth.

When the church service was over, they returned to Longbourn for a small gathering. All the ladies were exhausted, yet Elizabeth felt a small glimmer of relief. She had done what was right by her father, and she was very glad Lydia could be there to say one last goodbye.

"Elizabeth, Mr. Bingley and I have decided not to go directly to London." Jane sat down beside her sister. "We will miss this season's winter events and simply remain at Netherfield."

"Are you sure?"

"Quite sure. In my condition, Mr. Bingley believes I will have an easier and less stressful time remaining in the countryside." She smiled. "I must admit, I am glad of his decision."

"So am I." Elizabeth took her sister's hand. "It will be wonderful to have you around. I am still unsure how to handle Mamma. She is most reluctant to plan for leaving Longbourn, even though Mr. Collins is here every day trying to elicit her promise to quit the place."

"I have prepared quarters for you all at Netherfield. I wish she would just accept it and come."

"She cannot bear to give up her authority as the lady of the house. Gentleman's wife is the highest status Mamma has ever held, and it feels like her natural place in life now. Moving to the position of supported lodger feels like a sad state of affairs. I suppose I can understand it."

"Yes, of course. But we cannot change the facts of the matter. I hope Mamma will soon see reason."

Elizabeth agreed.

"Actually, I shall let Mr. Bingley know I plan to remain at Longbourn a while longer," Jane said, getting up. "We can sit together now for another hour or so, if you would like."

"I should like that very much, Jane."

Jane left the room, only to return a few minutes later. Her eyes shone brightly.

"Lizzy, you have a visitor."

"Is it Charlotte? Tell her I shall be down shortly. If she wants to take her husband away for a while, that would be much appreciated."

"It is not Mrs. Collins." Jane seemed to be quivering with some fresh information.

"Well, then who is it?"

"Mr. Darcy." Jane looked as though she might burst. "I really think you need to come and receive him, Lizzy."

Elizabeth got up and followed her sister downstairs. She was not really in the mood to receive guests, and particularly not the type of guest who made her feel deeply, as Mr. Darcy seemed to. She had resigned herself to avoiding him from now on, as she did not have the energy to handle both that and her grief.

"Miss Bennet." Mr. Darcy rose to greet her, and bowed gracefully. Mr. Collins was also in the room. He bowed flamboyantly, and said "Cousin. So nice to see you."

"I need to find my husband," Jane said. "And Mr. Collins, I understand you wish to locate your wife? Perhaps we shall walk together."

Mr. Collins nodded, and smiled his oily smile. "Of course. I am right behind you, dear eldest cousin."

"Please excuse us," Jane said. She closed the door behind them.

Elizabeth and Mr. Darcy were alone.

"Thank you," she said, before he could speak.

He was thrown somewhat off-course by this. "For what?"

"For everything. For finding Lydia. For keeping the matter confidential. Apparently, news of her potential compromise has not reached anyone. Your trustworthiness is valued and appreciated. We are all immensely grateful."

Mr. Darcy bowed slightly. "I thank you for your kind words. However, I have not come to reap your gratitude."

"No?"

"No. I have a more important matter to discuss."

Elizabeth looked at the man before her. His eyes twinkled in the firelight like dark gemstones. He was handsome, that was true. But he was somehow more than that. He was... What was he?

"Please, sit down." He guided her to a chair, then paced before her. She watched him, unsure where this was leading.

He stopped and looked out of the window for a second, as though gathering his thoughts. Then he fixed her with his dark eyes. She felt pinned to her chair by his attention. It was not an unpleasant sensation. On the contrary, she basked in the warmth of his gaze.

"Yes, Mr. Darcy?"

"Since the first moment we met, I have felt... an attachment to you."

Her mouth fell open a little.

He went on. "Your quick wit, your beauty, and your determination set you apart from any woman I have ever known. Nothing can stop you. Nobody can hold a candle to you. You are, quite simply, a queen among ladies."

Elizabeth remained speechless. She wondered if she was imagining the entire scene. But the tingling in her spine told her it was real.

"Miss Bennet, I must be frank with you. You deserve no less." He looked down at her hands in her lap, then back at her face. "I have never wanted to marry. I have never wanted a wife, or children, or to be the head of a household." He stepped forward and took her hands. "Until now."

"What…" Elizabeth stumbled over her words. "What are you saying, Mr. Darcy?"

"I am saying that I love you. With every fibre of my being, with every ounce of my heart, I love you. I have never in my life met somebody like you, and I never will again. If you do not feel anything for me, then I vow never to trouble you again. I will walk away at once. But if you do—" He kissed her hand. "If you feel even the slightest inclination towards me, then I beg you, Miss Bennet. Marry me."

Elizabeth could not speak for a second.

"Marry me, Miss Bennet. Be my wife. Make me the happiest man alive. I know you are in mourning, and we must observe the proper period of grief before we make any arrangements. But I can wait." He kissed her hand, with a tenderness she had never known. "I will wait until the ends of the earth if I have to."

Elizabeth laughed, with tears in her eyes.

"Well? What do you say?"

"For once in my life, I find it difficult to say anything."

"Then say yes. Say yes, you will marry me."

His face was now inches from hers. She gazed into his dark eyes and saw all the qualities she wanted in a husband. He was strong, and loving, and principled, and wise.

She loved him. She could not deny it.

"Yes," she whispered.

She could say no more, for then he took her in his arms and kissed her.

CHAPTER 28

ALMOST ONE YEAR LATER

Elizabeth bustled about Pemberley, checking that the greenery had been hung correctly. She directed a footman to adjust a sprig of mistletoe, and stood back to admire the result.

"Yes, that's perfect. Thank you, David."

"My pleasure, Mrs. Darcy."

Jane walked in, bobbing little Thomas in her arms. "I am just about to put your nephew to bed, Lizzy. Would you like a cuddle first?"

"I should love one," Elizabeth said, taking little Thomas gently in her arms.

"Mother is very happy in the blue guest room," Jane said, with a smile. "She thinks she has the most luxurious room in the whole house, and is writing letters to her friends in Hertford-shire telling them so."

"Well, she is right," Elizabeth said, kissing her nephew's soft cheek. "Nothing but the best for Mamma."

"It is so wonderful that she was able to stay at Longbourn after all. Thank heavens for your husband, Lizzy."

"I am amazed that Mr. Collins agreed to the transaction at all. But Charlotte says he was happy to take Mr. Darcy's offer, so it must have been a favourable one."

"I suspect your husband was extremely generous with him. He is a good man, Lizzy."

Elizabeth smiled at the thought of him. "He certainly is."

Loud laughter alerted them to the presence of their younger sisters. Mary, Kitty and Lydia fell into the room, giggling.

"Lizzy, may we see the guest list for tonight? We are all hoping to find ourselves fine young men to dance with."

"*You* are, you mean. I want no part of this." Mary folded her arms and looked disapproving.

Lydia and Kitty shrieked with laughter all the more.

"Of course, girls. The guest list is on the pianoforte. You may browse for your quarries there."

Jane took Thomas back from Elizabeth. He was already half-asleep, sucking his thumb.

"Oh, I forgot to tell you, Lizzy. Miss Bingley and the Hursts are unable to attend your ball tonight. They have a prior engagement for Twelfth Night in London, apparently."

The two sisters shared a smile. "What a terrible pity," said Elizabeth, drily. "I am sure we shall bear the disappointment."

"You sound like Father," Jane said. "Dear old father."

"He would have loved Thomas," Elizabeth said. "But let us not be sad today, Jane. It is a time of joy. It is Twelfth Night. There is much in the family to celebrate now."

"So there is, dear Lizzy."

Miss Carrington and Miss Darcy appeared in the room, arm-in-arm. The three unmarried Bennet sisters joined them happily.

"Oh, Miss Carrington! Is your fiancé able to attend tonight's festivities?" Elizabeth called.

"He is," Miss Carrington confirmed, radiant with pleasure. "His aunt and uncle will be in attendance, and they said they would bring him from Lincolnshire. I am looking forward to introducing him to you all."

"I should like that very much," Elizabeth said.

Jane returned, having put her baby boy to bed upstairs. She took Elizabeth's arm and drew her to one side.

"Lizzy… When you said there is much in the family to celebrate now, did you mean anything in particular?" She peered at Elizabeth, as though trying to read her expression.

"Perhaps," said Elizabeth, trying to keep a straight face. But she could not hide anything from her sister.

She placed her hands on her abdomen and raised her eyebrows at Jane.

Jane understood at once.

"Oh Lizzy, you're —" She clutched her heart, with an expression of rapture. "Are you and Mr. Darcy expecting your first child?"

"I think we are, Jane. Yes. I think we are."

Jane embraced her sister and squealed with joy.

"Oh, Lizzy. What a wonderful future you have."

Mr. Darcy chose the perfect moment to stroll

back in the room, flanked by Mr. Bingley. The two gentlemen took their wives' hands.

"Happy Twelfth Night, Mrs. Darcy," Mr. Darcy whispered into Elizabeth's ear.

"Happy future, Mr. Darcy," she whispered back.

"Always."

The two couples headed for the ballroom, to receive their guests.

THE END

ABOUT THE AUTHOR

Clara Winfield is an English author living in the Hertfordshire countryside with her very own Mr. Darcy and their two spirited children.

While studying for her English Literature degree, she fell in love with Jane Austen's world, and particularly with our dear couple, Miss Bennet and Mr. Darcy. She is honoured and privileged to write stories set in Miss Austen's richly-imagined world.

To Win A Frozen Heart is her debut novel.

clara@clarawinfield.com

NEW RELEASE MAILING LIST

To receive notification when I publish a new book, please join my mailing list:

Clara Winfield's Newsletter

Visit: http://eepurl.com/dhzyef

I promise only to contact you when I have a new book. Your email address will never be shared.

THANK YOU

Thank you for reading this book. I hope it succeeded in transporting you back in time, even if only fleetingly.

Writing in Miss Austen's world is a dream come true for me, and I am enormously grateful for the opportunity. Your support for my work means a great deal to me, and I appreciate it very much.

Clara Winfield
January 2018